I was halfway back to the surface when I realized that Shannon wasn't with me. Automatically assuming the worst, I hurried back down and saw her floating about two feet off the bottom at the very edge of the crater. She was almost motionless, and fear seized me for a moment. But then a long stream of bubbles poured out of her regulator and I knew she was breathing.

I swam closer, and a moment later I, too, was hanging motionless in the water. Directly under Shannon the bedrock changed colors—from gray to bronze. It was unreal. I knew what color that bronze would be at the surface. Gold. Pure gold.

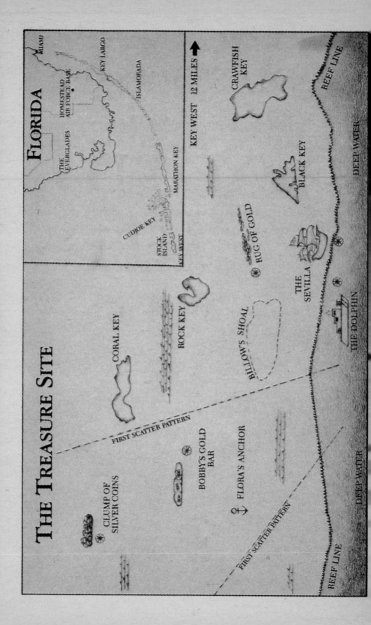

TODD STRASSER

BEYOND *the* REEF

Drawings by Debbe Heller

LAUREL-LEAF BOOKS

Published by
Dell Publishing
a division of
Bantam Doubleday Dell Publishing Group, Inc.
666 Fifth Avenue
New York, New York 10103

ISBN: 0-440-20881-5

RL: 5.5

Reprinted by arrangement with Delacorte Press

Printed in the United States of America

May 1991

10 9 8 7 6 5 4 3 2

OPM

To Geoff, our adventurer

BEYOND THE REEF

Sometimes I think back to when we led a normal life. We lived in Flintville, and my father was the Spanish teacher and swimming coach at Flintville High. My mother edited the women's page for the Flintville *Times Dispatch*. We lived in a white two-story house with a big front porch. In the winter I took the bus to school, and in the summer I went to the town camp at Hilltop Park. In the summer evenings we'd eat dinner on the screened-in porch, and then my friends and I would skateboard on the street or play laser tag through the backyards until it was too dark to see. I must have been nine or ten, and I had no complaints.

But that was a long time ago. I'm seventeen now, and Dad and I live in a leaky sailboat with a broken mast in the city marina of Key West, Florida. Dad says we've found over $1 million worth of sunken treasure in the last five years. Maybe he's right. But all I know is we're broke and living mostly on the money I make from selling stone crab claws. Mom's back in Flintville, and if things around here don't get better, I'll probably have to go back and live with her. I don't want to go, because Dad's in pretty bad shape, but I'm worried someone from school or the social services department is going to find out how we're living and send me away.

How did we wind up like this? I guess it all started with the trips we used to take each Easter vacation to visit Dad's parents in North Miami Beach. They loved to gamble, and spent most of their time at jai alai matches and the horse track at Hialeah. Sometimes they'd win and that night we'd go to a seafood restaurant for fried clams, shrimp, and lobster. But most of the time they lost, and we'd end up grilling hot dogs and playing hearts and poker while they waited for their next pension check to come. To tell you the truth, I didn't care whether they won or lost, because just being in warm, sunny Florida and away from cold, overcast Flintville was fun.

Whenever we visited, Dad and I would take off for a day and go fishing on a party boat out of Haulover Beach. You were supposed to catch yellowtail and snapper, but we mostly caught grunts, these inedible little brown fish that make this dumb grunting noise when you pull them out of the water. Since I was a kid I didn't care what I caught, but Dad would catch about twenty grunts and then lean his forearms on the boat's wooden railing and start grumbling about how someday we were going to go down to Key West and go for *real fish* like permit and tarpon. I didn't really believe him because that meant renting a car and paying for a motel room instead of staying at my grandparents' for free.

But one Easter Dad announced that we were actually going to go. When Mom asked how he planned to pay for it, he reminded her that he'd won nearly $600 in the New York Instant Lottery game the previous fall. Besides, he said, we'd only stay for one night. I could have sworn he'd already spent that $600 on a new clutch and brakes for our car, but Key West sounded cool so I kept my mouth shut.

We left Miami the next morning and drove south

on the turnpike. I sat in the back of the rented station wagon. In the front, Mom was quiet and I could tell that she was in a bad mood. I think she knew Dad had already spent the $600. Even though none of us had ever been south of Miami, she kept her nose stuck in a travel guide and hardly looked up.

After a while the highway narrowed, and we began to pass billboards advertising Mr. Submarine and Burger King and Captain Bob's Fish Market. Then the road narrowed again, this time to two lanes, and we started to pass brown swamps with strange gnarly trees whose twisting roots disappeared into the mud and brackish water. White egrets stood on the roots, and black birds hopped through the branches above. Twice we passed armadillos lying in the thin strip of grass by the side of the road, their shells crushed by cars. A sign said we were in Everglades National Park. Dad slowed the car and looked out his side window. Mom watched from hers too.

A few miles later we went over a steel drawbridge. A sign said we'd come to Key Largo, and we started passing marinas filled with white-hulled fishing boats and motels with names like The Sunset Reef and The Anchor Drop. The highway separated again. Tall palms, tamarinds with red-striped yellow flowers, and leafy rubber plants grew in the grassy median between the northbound and southbound lanes. We passed a shell shop with big piles of pink conches lying in the sun. To the left we could see the Straits of

Florida and to the right the Gulf of Mexico, both
bodies of water turning a dozen shades of turquoise
and blue as they spread out as far as the eye could
see. None of us had ever seen anything like this before, and even Mom rolled down her window to get a
better look. I knew from the map that we were on
the uppermost island in a thin chain that stretched
nearly a hundred miles to Key West. But no map
could've prepared us for how much water there was
or how different we felt surrounded by it.

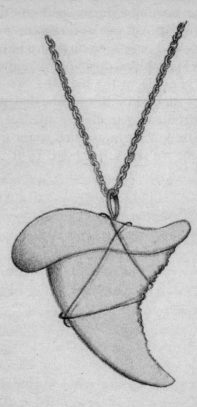

2

We checked into a motel in Key West that afternoon and set out to explore on foot. Soon we found ourselves in an old residential section with wooden houses and thick green foliage. As we walked down the cracked and broken sidewalks, we could hardly see some of the houses through the broad palms and tropical vegetation. Most were several stories tall, with peeling paint and shutters drawn tight against the glaring afternoon sun. Some had colorful fishing buoys or light-brown sponges hanging from their balconies.

The town itself was mostly bars, restaurants, and gift shops. Even in the middle of the afternoon the bars were filled with people drinking and listening to guitarists playing sixties folk and rock music. There must have been half a dozen stores that sold nothing but T-shirts. Dad bought sun screen in a gift shop that also sold plastic see-through bikinis.

"Key West is noted for its permissive atmosphere," Mom read from her travel guide.

We took a tour on the Conch Train, a little locomotive on tires that pulled open cars filled with tourists. We passed Ernest Hemingway's house, a giant banyan tree the size of a circus tent, and Sloppy Joe's bar, which had parachutes hanging from the ceiling. The tour guide told us that Key West used to be inhabited by pirates who'd put up false beacons at night to trick ships into smashing on the reefs. Then the pirates would row out the next day and plunder the ships.

"During the conquest of the New World," the tour guide continued, "numerous Spanish galleons sank in the waters around Key West. Historians estimate that more than three billion dollars' worth of gold and silver still lie on the sea bottom. Most of it in fifty feet of water or less."

Dad whistled and gave Mom a wide-eyed look. "Imagine that."

"Instead of fishing tomorrow, maybe you should go diving," Mom said, kidding him.

That evening we went to Mallory Square to watch the sun set. This was supposed to be the big daily event, and the square—it was actually a big concrete dock—was crowded with tourists. We got there early and wandered around jewelry stands, bought fresh fruit punch from a vendor, and watched jugglers and musicians perform.

One of the performers, a tall guy with a dark tan, had attracted a big crowd. He was wearing only a pair of cutoff jeans, and at his feet was a blanket covered with a thick layer of broken glass. When he said he was going to lie facedown on the glass and ask five tourists to stand on his back, I was certain it had to be a trick. But the next thing I knew, he lay down and had five men step onto his back and legs.

Gasps and murmurs ran through the crowd. "Is he bleeding?" "He must be nuts!" "How does he do that?"

I gave Dad a questioning glance, but he shook his head and whispered, "Don't ask me."

The men got off and the guy jumped up and faced the crowd with his arms outspread. Pieces of broken glass clung to his chest and thighs, but we couldn't find a single cut. Everyone clapped and stuffed dollar bills into a hat he passed around.

"Not a bad living," Dad observed.

"You could say he's on the cutting edge of entertainment," Mom added dryly.

Nearby, a tall woman with a long blond ponytail was selling pink coral necklaces and shark-teeth pendants. I really wanted to go back to Flintville with a shark's tooth hanging from a chain around my neck.

"I'm having a half-off sale today," the woman told me as I stared at the teeth.

"Can I get one, Dad?" I asked eagerly. "Please? They're half off."

Dad smiled. "I get the feeling they're half off every day."

I wasn't exactly thrilled by the idea of watching the sun go down. But hanging in the western sky over a small island, it looked bigger and more orange than I'd ever seen it. Sailboats floated in the sparkling orange reflection and sea gulls glided in the air. Above us wispy streaks of clouds glowed pink against the deepening blue sky. The whole thing sort of reminded me of a postcard. Even the vendors stopped and watched. When the sun finally sank behind the island, everyone cheered.

After dinner at a seafood place that offered all the fried shrimp and clams you could eat, we walked back to the motel. The night air was warm and moist and smelled earthy, like the terrarium we had at school. The sky was filled with stars, and clouds of flying insects fizzed under the streetlights. People on bikes passed us at a leisurely pace, as if they were just out for an evening spin. I couldn't recall seeing anyone that day who'd seemed particularly rushed.

Later, as we stood in the light outside our motel-room door, waiting for Dad to get the key to work, Mom suddenly gasped, "What is that!?" and pointed at a flat brown beetle about the size of a small mouse ambling across the asphalt.

"That, I believe, is what they call a palmetto bug," Dad said.

"Wanna squash it?" I asked.

Dad looked at the beetle and then at me. "Better live and let live," he said. I guess he thought he was espousing a basic Key West philosophy, but I, frankly, was disappointed.

3

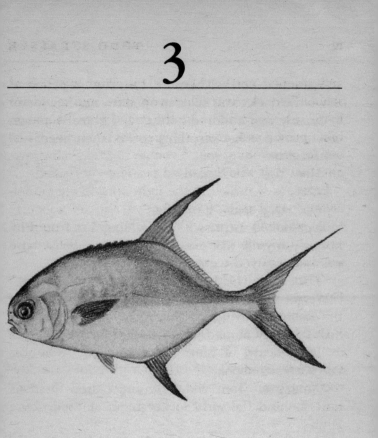

The next morning we met Tom, our fishing guide. He was a big man in khaki pants and a matching shirt, with wild sun-streaked brown hair and a bushy beard. His lips were cracked and chapped from too much sun, and he had zinc oxide on his reddened nose.

"Where're you folks from?" he asked as he led us down the dock to his boat, an open twenty-five footer with a big two-hundred-horsepower Merc. A couple of pelicans perched on pilings cocked their heads and watched us.

"New York," Dad said.

"City?"

"No," Dad said. "Flintville."

Tom looked surprised. "No kidding. I'm from Philipsburg myself, just over the mountain. What business you say you were in?"

"Education," Dad said. "I teach at Flintville High."

We got in the boat and Tom motored slowly out of the marina, obeying the "No Wake" signs. "You ever hear of a guy named Joe Piattoni?" he asked.

"Ever heard of him?" Dad laughed. "Son-of-a-gun's my principal."

"Amazing," Tom said. "He and I used to sneak butts behind the girls' locker room at Philipsburg High."

They shared a couple of laughs about Flintville and Philipsburg and then Dad asked, "What brought you down here?"

"Came down for vacation once," Tom said.

"And you liked it?"

"Hell, yes." Tom snorted. "I never went back."

We got past the no-wake zone and Tom told us to sit on the cushions in front of the steering console. Then he opened that Merc up. The engine whined and the boat rose and planed the surface of the water. Dad and I grabbed our caps and held on tight as we headed west with the morning sun at our backs, the wind in our faces, and turquoise water all around.

We spent the morning fishing for permit, a flat, silvery fish about the size of a snowshoe and with the strength of a thousand grunts. Tom baited our hooks with crabs and Dad and I stood in the boat, rocking slightly, the coconut smell of suntan lotion filling our noses. After a while there'd be a flash in the water as if someone had tilted a mirror into the sun, and then one of our rods would bend double as line started to scream off the reel. The fish would fight for fifteen or twenty minutes, and each time I'd bring him close to the boat he'd turn and streak away. By the time Tom leaned over the side and grabbed the exhausted fish by the tail, I was nearly exhausted too.

Just before lunch I hooked what felt like the biggest permit of the day. He must've run from the boat six times before I finally brought him alongside. Tom kneeled over the gunwale, waiting for me to bring him closer. The permit lay on its side on the surface, its gills flapping up and down.

"What do you think he weighs?" I asked excitedly.

"About eighteen pounds," Tom said, reaching for the line. "Now bring your rod tip slowly toward me."

Before I could, the permit suddenly splashed and ran again. Tom jumped up, looking alarmed.

"What is it?" Dad asked.

"There." Tom pointed about fifty feet from the boat. A huge yellow blur shot through the water following my line. The permit raced away, but it was no match for the blur. A moment later my line went slack. There was nothing on the other end.

"What happened?" I asked.

"Bull shark," Tom said grimly. "Probably about four hundred pounds."

I have to admit I was pretty depressed as I reeled my slack line in. Dad gave me a consolatory pat on the head.

"That happen much?" he asked Tom.

"All the time," Tom said. "Shark'll take a tired, crippled fish over a healthy one anytime he can."

After lunch we headed for another spot to catch snappers for dinner. I could see Dad was really enjoying himself. After all those years of catching grunts, we were finally going for the best sport and eating fish in the world. This was the ultimate.

We had just reached the next spot when a new sound met our ears, a distant *whop, whop, whop* that grew steadily louder until a helicopter appeared and shot past us. I could tell by the way Tom watched it that helicopters weren't something you saw a lot of in the Gulf of Mexico.

"Betcha someone's found something," he said,

reaching into the console and pulling out a pair of binoculars.

"Like what?"

"Sunken treasure." Tom focused the binoculars on the horizon. "A crew of divers've been working this area for a couple of months now."

Dad was instantly on his feet, shielding his eyes from the sun and trying to squint into the distance. Tom started to hand him the binoculars. "Want a look?"

"Why not go see for ourselves?" Dad asked.

Tom tugged on his beard, probably a little surprised that Dad was so eager to give up any part of our fishing time. "Okay, why not?"

Ten minutes later we found a dozen boats floating in a loose circle around a big old cabin cruiser and a vessel that looked like a tugboat. Both were dirty and rusted, with frayed ropes and dented bumpers hanging off the sides. Deckhands with sun-bleached hair and sun-browned skin were busy filling diving tanks and lowering metal baskets over the sides of both ships. Overshadowing everything was the loud *whop, whop* of the helicopter hovering practically on top of us, whipping up everyone's hair and churning the water around the boats. A photographer was belted in the open door of the copter, aiming a camera with a telescopic lens.

Suddenly a diver wearing a mask and tank broke

the surface of the water between the two vessels. Everyone on board dropped what they were doing. On our boat, Dad pressed the binoculars to his eyes. The diver lifted one hand in the air and I saw something sparkle in the sunlight. He lifted the other hand, but I couldn't see what it held. The deckhands began to shout and cheer.

"What's he got?" Tom asked.

"Looks like a gold chain," Dad said. "But I never saw one so thick."

"What's in the other hand?" I asked eagerly.

"Can't tell."

We watched the diver give his finds to one of the hands on the tug and then dive again. Two more divers splashed into the water behind him. Tom picked up his boat radio. "Hey, Mort, it's Tom. What's he got?"

"Looks like eight foot of gold chain," the radio crackled back. *"And an emerald about the size of a man's thumb."*

Tom whistled between his teeth. "Guess they'll be eatin' porterhouse tonight, huh?"

"And for a long time to come."

"Okay, thanks."

"Sure thing." The radio crackled off.

"Who's that?" I asked.

"Captain of one of the other boats," Tom said.

Dad was sitting at the console, rocking gently with the boat and looking a little dazed. "A gold chain that big must weigh at least five pounds," he said. "At four hundred an ounce, that's *thirty thousand dollars*."

"I'd take that emerald," Tom said. "They got one about the size of a piece of bubble gum last week. Figured its value at over fifty thousand."

"Then we just saw nearly a hundred thousand in treasure," Dad said, awestruck.

We fished for snapper that afternoon, but Dad spent most of the time in a daze. At one point the tip of his rod started jerking wildly, but he just sat there, staring off into the sky.

"Hey, Dad? Dad!"

"Huh?" He blinked. "What?"

"You've got a fish."

"Oh, yeah." Dad started reeling it up. I couldn't remember seeing him act this weird before. I glanced over at Tom, but he just looked amused, as if we were figuring out something he'd known for a long time.

Later, back at the marina, Mom was waiting for us. We said good-bye to Tom and walked along the wooden dock toward the parking lot.

"Have a good time?" she asked me as we passed the skiffs and fishing boats bobbing gently in their berths.

"Great," I said. "We caught a ton of fish and watched this diver bring up treasure."

"Really?" Mom's eyebrows rose as if she thought

my boyish imagination was running wild. But Dad backed me up.

"It was unbelievable," he said.

Other charter boats were coming in and we stopped to watch them unload grouper, dorado, and kingfish.

"How about you, Mom?" I asked.

"Oh, I had the most fascinating day," Mom said. "The history here is simply incredible. And the writers. Not just Ernest Hemingway. Tennessee Williams lived here, and John Dos Passos. Alison Lurie comes every year to write . . ."

The station wagon was waiting in the dirt parking lot, already packed for the trip back to Miami. Mom and Dad stopped and stared at our suitcases in the back as if they couldn't believe we were really going to leave. Mom looked up at the sun, already starting to turn orange and sink toward the horizon. Dad looked back at the fishing boats. Pelicans sat on the pilings by the dock, and a yellow dog lay in the long late-afternoon shadow of the bait shack. I knew how my parents felt. There was something about Key West. I couldn't explain it, but I could feel it. It was the orange sun, the turquoise water, and the green palms. It was places like Mallory Square at sunset and the guy who made his living lying on a bed of glass. It was the easy pace, gift shops that sold see-through bikinis, and restaurants with all the fried shrimp you could eat.

Also, it wasn't Flintville, which suddenly seemed awfully boring.

"What do you say we stay another night?" Dad asked.

"Just what I was thinking," said Mom.

4

It was on the jet back to New York that they decided to move. They made me promise to keep it a secret until Dad gave notice at the end of the school year. Mom quit the newspaper a few weeks later. They put the house on the market and had a couple of garage sales to get rid of all the furniture and junk they didn't want. What they didn't sell they stored with Mom's parents, who also lived in Flintville. In Key West, Mom was going to write a novel and Dad was going to hunt for treasure.

Key West was a lot hotter in August than it had been over Easter vacation. Almost every afternoon the temperature hit the upper nineties or low one hundreds. Even the shade was hot. It was quiet too. A lot of the stores were closed and people were away. "Up north" was the usual answer if you asked where they'd gone. Fortunately Dad had kept in touch with Tom over the summer, and he came around to say hello and show us a few tricks. Like which air-conditioned restaurants would cook up a meal cheap if we brought our own fish.

We moved into a house on Ashe Street that was about a third the size of our old house back in Flintville. The tiny front yard was filled with palms, vines, and hibiscus. From the sidewalk you let yourself through a squeaky wooden gate and followed a short path made of cinder blocks up to a small screened porch. Except the screen was old and rusty and filled with hundreds of holes that let bugs in. The house was painted dark blue on the outside. Inside, the four rooms were varying shades of yellow. The living room was just large enough for a couch, a coffee table, and a TV in the corner. The kitchen had an old curvy-cornered refrigerator that grumbled all the time and a gas stove you had to light with a match. In the back were two small bedrooms, separated by the bathroom. No bathtub, just a drippy shower with mold growing on the tiles, a toilet, and a little sink like the ones in restaurant bathrooms. The small yard in the back was overgrown with shrubs and weeds. When we first looked at it Mom called it "quaint." When the landlord told him the rent Dad called it "outrageous." After living there for a week we all called it "the Shack."

Within weeks Dad got his diving certification and bought an old fishing boat with some of the money from our house up north. Her windows were tinted Coke-bottle green and her smokestack belched sooty black smoke whenever Dad started her up. He named her the *Treasure Hunter*. Mom worked on her novel every morning and explored the island on her bike in the afternoons. Bikes were the most popular means of transportation in Key West. Dad sold our car and got us all "conch cruisers" with fat, balloon tires, high handlebars, and plastic milk crates tied on the back for carrying stuff.

School hadn't started yet so I worked on the boat with Dad and explored a little with Mom. In the back of my mind I kept wondering what the Horace O'Bryant Middle School would be like and whether I'd fit in. I was twelve and going into the sixth grade, and I was always on the lookout for kids my own age.

The kid I saw most often was the girl who lived next door to us in a house about the same size as the Shack. She had a long blond ponytail and usually wore T-shirts and pastel-colored surfer trunks. If she'd been a guy, I probably would have gotten friendly right away, but since she was a girl, I wasn't as interested.

One day, though, the chain came off my bike. I was squatting on the curb, trying to get it back on, when I heard someone say, "Need some help?"

I turned around and found her twisting the end of her ponytail in her fingers. She had blue eyes and sun-bleached eyebrows and her skin was caramel-colored from the sun.

"Thanks, but I think I can manage," I said.

"You just moved in, right?" she said.

"Yeah. My name's Chris Cooper. What's yours?"

"Shannon Horn. Where'd you come from?"

I told her about Flintville and how we'd moved down so Dad could dive for treasure. Shannon didn't seem surprised. She acted like hunting for treasure was a normal everyday occupation in Key West. She told me she'd lived there since she was two years old.

"So you're sort of a native," I said.

"A conch?" Shannon replied, now looking surprised. "No way."

"What's a conch?" I asked.

"People who've lived here a long time," she explained. "It's spelled c-o-n-c-h, but they pronounce it 'conk.' I mean, you can't be a conch unless your grandfather was born and died here."

"So where're you from?" I asked.

"Well, it's me and my mom," Shannon said. "She's from Ohio, but I was born on a commune in Virginia."

"What's your mom do?"

"She sells coral necklaces and shark's teeth at Mallory Square. You've probably seen her. If you look interested, she usually says she's having a half-off sale."

"Yeah." I grinned. "Across from the guy who lies on glass."

Shannon nodded and walked around to the front of the bike. I guess she'd noticed I wasn't making much progress with the chain. "Let me hold the back wheel up," she said. "Then it'll be easier to turn the pedal and get the chain on the sprocket."

I knew she was right and let her hold the bike while I got the chain on. Then I went back into my house and washed the grease off my hands. When I came back out Shannon was still there. I guess neither of us had anything important to do. I wasn't real comfortable with the idea of making friends with a girl, but on the other hand, kids weren't exactly breaking down the door to meet me.

"So, uh, what do you do around here?" I asked.

"Well, crawfish season just opened and we could get some cowhide for my traps."

"Crawfish? Cowhide?"

"You probably call 'em lobster. The cowhide is bait."

"What do you do with them?" I asked.

Shannon gave me a funny look. I guess the answer was pretty obvious. "Sell 'em, what else?"

We spent the afternoon in Shannon's boat baiting wooden traps with scraps of cowhide and sinking them in places where Shannon thought the crawfish were plentiful. She had her own fourteen-foot fiberglass skiff with a twenty-five-horsepower Yamaha she'd bought with money from selling lobster and stone crab claws. "A lot of kids around here fish commercially," she said. "I'm gonna be a trawler captain when I'm older."

"Your mom doesn't mind if you take the boat out alone?" I asked.

"Why should she?"

"I don't know. I guess 'cause you're only twelve. I don't think my parents would let me."

"My mom thinks it's great," Shannon said. "She says as long as I make money selling crawfish and stone crab claws, she doesn't have to give me an allowance."

I smiled. "Never thought of it that way."

5

Even though she was a girl, Shannon and I became
friends. I helped her tend her crawfish traps and she
took me to Smather's Beach, where we went rafting
and "skimboarding." She even introduced me to
some of the other kids there, so by the time school
started I didn't feel so much like a stranger.

By the spring I hardly even thought about
Flintville anymore. My skin was tan, and I'd gotten
Mom to buy me colored T-shirts and surfer shorts so
I'd fit in with the other kids. Even the words I used
changed. I no longer said "sneakers, soda, and hero
sandwich." Now I said "tennis shoes, pop, and submarine." Shannon was still my closest friend, and I'd
even gotten used to the fact that she was a girl.

Things weren't going as well for my parents. Mom
lost interest in her book and ran out of places to
explore. Often I'd come home from school and find
her staring at the TV in the living room. Dad had
started treasure hunting in earnest and found old
shopping carts, broken engine props, and hundreds
of beer cans. About the only thing of value he found
was a big Penn deep-sea fishing reel some charter
boat must have lost. The gears were a little rusty, but
he was able to fix it up. He said he could sell it for
$200, but he never did. It stayed in the closet instead.

I think Dad was surprised at how hard treasure
hunting was. At first I went with him almost every
chance I could, but he said I was too young to dive
and it got boring sitting in the boat all day while he
motored back and forth, studying charts and watching his electronic instruments for a sign of something
interesting on the bottom. Some of the local resi-
dents made it hard on him too. When we stopped in
the marina office to pay for fuel and get supplies, the
charter-boat captains would shake their heads and

mumble behind his back. I once heard one of them say something about the "fool snowbird treasure hunter."

Even Mr. Carroll, my teacher at school, made fun of him.

"Chris Cooper?" he called one morning during attendance.

"Here," I said.

He paused from his attendance book and looked up at me. "I hear your father thinks he's a treasure hunter, Chris. Tell us, what valuable treasure has he wrested from the bottom of the sea this week?"

Suddenly the whole class was staring at me, giggling. I felt my face turn red. "Nothing, Mr. Carroll."

At home the tension between Mom and Dad was ever-present. Mom seemed especially irritable. One evening I was doing my homework at the kitchen table with my feet up on the chair across from me. I noticed her looking at my tennis shoes.

"How long have you had a hole in your sneaker?" she asked.

"I don't know," I said, although the truth was it had been there for weeks. In fact, I'd noticed that day that I could see clear through to my right big toe.

Just then the screen door slammed, and Dad came in lugging a greasy piece of metal that looked like part of an engine. His hair was wild and stringy. He hadn't cut it since we'd moved. He had a beard too. A bushy one like Tom's.

"Look at your son's sneaker," Mom said, without even saying hello.

Dad put the part down on the table and looked at my right tennis shoe. "I'll patch it after dinner."

"Does he have to go to school with patched sneakers?" Mom asked. "Can't we afford a new pair?"

Dad rubbed his hand across his forehead, leaving a greasy black smudge. "Don't start with me, Ann. I've had enough today."

"What happened?" I asked.

"Some idiot put sugar in the *Treasure Hunter*'s gas tank," he said. "I had to dump fifty gallons of diesel and this carburetor's still gummed up."

Mom turned and saw the carburetor. "You're getting grease all over the table!"

"Cool off," Dad grumbled as he picked up the carburetor and moved it out to the porch. He was always leaving things around the house, which made Mom mad of course. Eventually he'd move them out to the porch, which was now littered with cans of motor oil and marine paint, brushes, engine parts, and other odds and ends. Anything that proved to be unsalvageable wound up in a heap in the backyard.

He came back in and looked at my tennis shoe again. "It's fine except for the toe. Stupid to go out and buy a new pair."

"I don't want my son going to school looking like a bum," Mom snapped. "It's bad enough *you* go around looking the way you do."

Dad stared at her, rubbing his face with his hands again, leaving more grease marks. "I just dumped seventy-five bucks' worth of diesel in the ocean. If I have to get that carburetor rebuilt, it's gonna run at least two hundred. Maybe I don't happen to have an extra sixty dollars right now for a damn pair of sneakers."

"Do you have to swear in front of him?" Mom growled through clenched teeth.

"Well, don't give me such a hard time about money," Dad growled back.

Mom turned and wiped her hands on a dish towel. "You seem to have plenty of it for that stupid boat."

Dad glared at her, his face turning red. He slammed his fist down on the table, making the plates rattle.

"You don't understand *anything,* you know that?" he shouted. "It takes money to run a boat. I've got diesel to pay for, compressed air, insurance, repairs, dock fees. Even the graph paper for the depth finder is expensive. And on top of everything some jackass pours sugar in my tank. Now what am I supposed to do about that?"

"You *could* find some treasure," Mom replied snidely.

"You think I'm not trying?" Dad shouted, the veins in his neck sticking out. "I'm in that boat twelve hours a day in all kinds of weather. You think it's fun being out there in a squall with six-foot waves break-ing over the bow?"

"Well, do you think it's fun sitting around this house all day waiting to cook you dinner?" Mom shouted back, her face as red as his.

Dad stopped and looked stunned. "What's that got to do with anything?"

"Everything!" Mom shrieked. She stormed out of the kitchen and slammed the bedroom door. We could hear her sobbing.

Dad slid his hands into his pockets and looked glum. Five hamburgers were sizzling in a pan on the stove. "You better take care of dinner, Chris," he said, and went into the bedroom.

After eating two burgers I cleaned off a spot at the table and tried to get back to my homework. But it was hard to concentrate. I could hear my parents in the bedroom, no longer shouting, but talking as if they were trying to work things out. What Mom had said before about cooking dinner seemed to come straight out of left field, but the more I thought about it, the more it made sense. It wasn't the hole in my tennis shoe that upset her as much as what it repre-sented. Up north I'd never had holes in my sneakers, Dad had never brought greasy engine parts into the house, and Mom never had to sit around all day with nothing to do except wait for us to come home.

Later Dad came back into the kitchen and took a

beer out of the refrigerator. He leaned against the door, looking grim.

"How are things at school, Chris?"

"Okay."

"Anyone giving you a hard time?"

I shook my head. I didn't consider Mr. Carroll a hard time, just a minor pain.

"You know, they didn't just put sugar in the *Treasure Hunter*'s tank," Dad said. "They crossed out *Treasure* on the stern and painted in *Garbage*."

"*Garbage Hunter*?" I winced.

"I mentioned it because it seemed like the kind of thing kids would do," Dad said.

"Not anyone I know," I said.

Dad nodded and glanced at my tennis shoes. "Tomorrow, after school, we'll get you a new pair. Don't let me forget."

A few weeks later they decided that Mom would get a job to tide us over until Dad started finding emeralds and gold chains on the sea bottom. The problem was, there were no newspaper or writing jobs in Key West. The only job available was waitressing.

One day I came home from school and found her standing in front of the mirror in the bedroom pinning her hair up. She was wearing a white blouse, a black skirt, and black stockings. Because she'd had some experience in college and was a little older than the average waitress, she was able to get a job at the Pier House, a fancy resort near Mallory Square.

"First night, huh?" I said, sitting down on the bed behind her. I have to admit I was looking forward to this new arrangement. Things had gotten so tense between her and Dad, and the Shack was so small, that I sometimes felt like we were living on top of a neutron bomb.

"I don't believe I'm doing this, Chris," Mom said, with her lips pressed around a couple of bobby pins. Even though she was forty, she was still slim and pretty, with soft shoulder-length black hair and dark eyebrows and eyes. I knew kids whose mothers were younger but who'd gotten fat and wore the same blue or yellow polyester shorts and matching shirts for days on end.

"You'll do fine," I said, thinking she needed encouragement.

"I know I'll do fine," she said curtly as she stuck another pin into her hair. "That's not the point."

"Then what's the point?" I asked.

She turned and looked at me, her eyes a little watery. For a moment I thought she might cry.

"Oh, I don't know, Chris," she said. "I guess I'm just mad that things haven't worked out the way I'd hoped."

"You mean with your novel?"

"That and other things. Life down here isn't what I

expected, and your father . . ." She didn't finish the sentence.

"What, Mom?"

She shook her head. Now I was certain she needed encouragement.

"Don't worry. Dad's bound to find something," I said. "We even read about it in school. Hundreds of galleons sank on the reefs. There must be tons of treasure down there."

Mom gave me a weak smile, the one that said, *You don't understand, but it doesn't matter because you're only a kid.*

"Maybe we made a mistake, Chris," she said sadly. "Maybe we shouldn't have left Flintville after all."

6

Life calmed down after that. Five nights a week Mom worked late, and even though she wasn't crazy about waitressing, I think she enjoyed having something to do and money to spend. We got through the summer without any more vandalism to the *Treasure*

Hunter, and suddenly it was fall again and I was back in school.

One afternoon I was sitting at the kitchen table doing my homework when the screen door banged open and Dad rushed in carrying a dripping burlap sack. He had a crazy grin on his face and a wild look in his eyes. His hair was spiky and stiff with dried salt water, and his boat clothes were stained and smelled of diesel fuel.

"Clear that stuff off the table," he ordered.

I managed to get my books off just as he dropped the sack with a thump. A couple of sand fleas fell out of the fibers and kicked helplessly in the little puddles on the tabletop. Dad pulled the sack open, revealing a wet, blackened hunk about the size of a toolbox. It looked a little like a big loaf of bread that had been scorched in the oven.

"What is it?" I asked.

"Silver coins," Dad announced gleefully. "Hundreds of silver coins fused and corroded together by time and the sea."

I stared at the hunk and then at him. This is it, I thought. He's finally flipped.

Dad must've read my mind, because he turned the hunk around and showed me a place where he'd scraped the blackened surface away. Underneath, it did look as if a bunch of silver coins had fused together. I reached forward and touched it. It felt cold and wet and metallic. Some of the black stuff came off on my fingers.

"This is it, Chris!" Dad practically shouted. "The day we've been waiting for!" He was like a madman. He'd sit at the table and stare at the hunk for a few moments. Then he'd jump up and start pacing around the kitchen, throwing punches in the air like a boxer pumping himself up for a big fight. He even called Mom at the Pier House and told her to come home right away.

"I did it!" he kept saying. "I knew I'd find it. And this is just the start!"

Ten minutes later the front door flew open and Mom dashed in. I guess Dad hadn't been too clear on the phone and she thought it was an emergency.

"What happened?" she shouted. "Is everybody okay?"

"Look!" Dad pointed at the black hunk on the kitchen table.

"What?" she gasped. "What is it?"

"Silver," Dad said.

Mom scowled at the thing. Then she looked at Dad and started backing away. She motioned for me to get up. "I think you better go to Shannon's, Chris," she said softly.

"No, wait! Look!" Dad showed her the scraped spot.

Mom bent down for a closer look. She squinted at

it, then touched it with her finger. She looked up at
Dad. "You think?"

"I know," Dad said with a huge grin. "I swear, hon,
it's real!"

The next thing I knew Mom let out a *whoop!* and
jumped into his arms. They started dancing around
the kitchen table, singing. They've *both* gone nuts, I
thought.

Later Dad went to the hardware store and came
back with two big galvanized tubs, a couple of gallons
of acid, a battery charger, some wire, and alligator
clips. He placed the hunk of coins in one of the tubs
and immersed it in the acid. By then Tom had arrived with a bottle of champagne, and Shannon and
her mother, Betty, brought brownies. Dad turned
the radio on and we had a party.

"Here's to the first of many finds," Tom toasted,
holding up a coffee mug filled with champagne.
Shannon, Betty—who didn't drink alcohol—and I
toasted with ginger ale in our mugs.

"See? You ought to have more faith, hon," Dad
said, putting his arm around Mom's shoulders. Mom's
smile was a little crooked.

We stayed up pretty late that night. Betty and
Shannon left, but Tom stayed and sat with us at the
kitchen table. Around midnight Mom made him
some coffee.

"It ain't just the treasure that's important," he said

as he poured some sugar into his cup and stirred it. "You're proving to the conchs that a stranger can come down here and succeed. I'm still trying to convince them you don't need to be born in the Keys to be a decent guide. These conchs are good people, but they've been burned too many times. They've seen real estate developers come in and change their town, mess up their sewer and water systems. They've got parades of kids jamming Duval Street every Saturday night. People come down here saying they can guide and it turns out they don't know a gaff from a push pole."

"I've noticed they can be pretty unsociable," Dad said, glancing at me. I knew he was thinking about the sugar in the *Treasure Hunter*'s tanks.

"Well, hell, it ain't their fault," Tom said. "Guys come down here to hunt treasure. They wind up charging a lot of fuel and supplies, and when they don't find anything they just take off in the middle of the night and leave the merchants high and dry. What do you expect?"

Dad didn't answer. He tilted his chair back and sipped some champagne. Tom drank his coffee. A mosquito had gotten through the screen and was buzzing in my ear, so I swatted it.

"If it's that hard, Tom, what keeps you down here?" Mom asked.

Tom shrugged. "Guess I love what I'm doing. And maybe I feel like I got something to prove, that not every stranger who comes down here is a fool and a liar."

They were still talking when I went to bed around 1:00 A.M. Early the next morning I woke to the sound of something going *thunk, thunk, thunk.* Rubbing my eyes, I wandered into the kitchen and found Dad sitting at the table tapping one corner of the hunk with a leather mallet. As I watched, a few of the coins came loose, but they were still covered with a dull gray film.

"Gold can sit on the bottom of the ocean forever and still be as shiny as the day it was minted," he said, picking up the loose coins. "But sea salt turns silver black. This'll get the last of the salts and corrosion off." He attached each loose coin to an alligator clip hanging from a wire in the second galvanized tub. The tub was filled with an electrolytic solution and hooked up to the battery charger. Then he sat down and started tapping again.

Over the next two days Dad separated and cleaned all the coins. I'd never seen him so absorbed. If Mom hadn't put sandwiches in front of him, I'm not sure he would've eaten.

Even cleaned and shiny, the coins weren't what I'd expected. They came in as many strange shapes as the chocolate-chip cookies Mom and I used to make at home. Dad said this was because in the old days all coins were struck by hand. Many were so badly corroded that he couldn't read the dates, but near the center of the hunk he found about a dozen coins dated 1632. The next morning he took the bus to Miami to have a coin expert look at them.

Two days later I came home from school and found him sitting in the living room reading the instructions for a new piece of equipment. He'd gotten a haircut and his beard was trimmed and he was wearing a clean shirt and pants.

"What'd they say?" I asked.

"Authentic pieces of eight." Dad grinned. "And I got a good price."

"You *sold* 'em?"

"Well sure, Chris," Dad said. "We needed the money. Besides, there's plenty more where they came from."

I believed him, but I was still shocked that he'd sold the coins so quickly. I guess I'd always thought that the idea of finding treasure was to keep it. On the other hand, I was excited by the idea of finding more.

"You should teach me to dive," I said. "Then we'll find twice as much treasure."

Dad just nodded and looked back down at the instructions. "Soon, Chris, soon."

A few moments later Mom came in. It was time for her to go to work. Dad told her he'd sold the coins.

"Can we start looking for a new place to live?" she asked. The night before she'd awakened in the dark to find a palmetto bug crawling up her arm, and now she was determined to move.

Dad blinked. "Well, I had to buy some things."

"Like what?" Mom asked.

"An air compressor, a couple of new regulators, and a high-speed magnetometer, which'll make it a lot easier to find more coins."

"But there must be some money left," Mom said.

"Well, uh, actually I had to borrow a little to get the magnetometer," Dad admitted. "But I showed the salesman the coins and he said he'd be glad to stake me."

Mom's face turned hard. I thought she was going to scream, but she glanced at me and then marched into the bedroom. It was pretty obvious that she wanted to talk to Dad in private. He got up and followed her, closing the door behind him. But in the living room I could still hear everything.

"How could you do that?" Mom demanded. "You know I can't stand living here. The refrigerator keeps conking out, the bathroom is disgusting, at night I lie in bed waiting for some creature to crawl over me."

"Don't you see that this'll save us money?" Dad asked, trying to reason with her. "Now I won't have to pay the dive shop for air, and I'll be able to find treasure twice as fast as before."

"You and your stupid treasure!" Mom's voice rose.

"Meanwhile, your son and wife suffer while you chase this idiotic dream."

"You call those coins *a dream*?" Dad shouted. "You know what the dealer in Miami told me? There's no record of a ship from 1632 being lost in these waters. As far as anyone knows, the whole treasure fleet of 1632 was captured by the Dutch. That means there's a treasure ship out there no one's discovered yet."

"That's right," Mom shouted back, "and *you* haven't discovered it either!"

I couldn't stand listening to them and went out the front door. But outside, I could still hear it. Maybe Shannon was home. When I knocked on her door Betty opened it, almost as if she'd been expecting me.

"Come in, Chris," she said sympathetically. It was obvious that she'd heard the fight too. As usual, she was wearing a faded work shirt and jeans. I noticed she was barefoot.

"Shannon around?" I asked gloomily.

"She went down to Che Che's to get some bread, but she should be back soon," Betty said. "I hope you won't mind, but I was in the middle of meditating."

"Is it okay if I wait?"

"Sure." Betty went into the living room and sat down on a straw mat. She crossed her legs and placed her palms upward on her knees and closed her eyes. Across from her was a large worktable covered with tools, scraps of silver, and jars of coral beads.

I went into the kitchen. Betty had a lot of hanging plants in her kitchen, along with spice racks filled with herbs she cooked with. On the table were a couple of pamphlets with titles like *The Divine Path* and *The Spiritual Aspect of the Vegetarian Diet*. I could still hear my parents yelling next door, but I tried not to listen. Through the doorway to the living room I could see Betty fidget a little. It must have been a challenge to try to meditate through all that racket.

Something in our house crashed, and Betty opened her eyes. My parents were too noisy to allow her to meditate after all. She got up, went to her worktable, and began drilling holes through shark's teeth with a small jeweler's drill.

"Sometimes I just feel like running away," I said, coming out of the kitchen.

"That's understandable," said Betty.

"You think I should?"

"No. It would only make things worse."

"But it's so selfish," I said. "All they can think about is themselves."

Betty gazed pensively out the window. The afternoon sun was shining through a piece of stained glass, turning parts of her face red, yellow, and green. "They have their own lives to think about, Chris. If they're unhappy, they have to deal with it. Once they do, they won't be so selfish."

I guess I knew she was right. Just because they

were my parents didn't mean they couldn't have their own problems. Betty started on another shark's tooth.

"Where do you get them?" I asked.

"Funny you should ask. I used to get them from Captain Bob, but his wife saw how well they sold and decided to go into the jewelry business for herself. This is all I've got left."

Next door my parents were still fighting. This had to be the marathon argument of the year. Suddenly I had an idea. "If I got you some teeth, would you pay me?"

"Sure, I'll give you two dollars a tooth."

"How about four dollars?" I said.

Betty looked up at me and smiled. "Three dollars. But they've got to be big ones."

"It's a deal."

7

The next day I caught up with Shannon at lunch. She was sitting with a couple of girls, so I didn't join her. I just stood across the table until she looked up and noticed me.

"Oh, hi," she said with a smile.

"Hi, Shan, think I could borrow your skiff?" Shannon's friends looked up and sort of smiled at me. I sort of smiled back.

"Why?" Shannon asked.

"Just feel like doing some fishing."

"Okay, but remember to fill the tank."

"Thanks, Shan."

I took my tray to another table and sat down. I'd been late getting to the cafeteria, and most of the kids had already eaten and were outside playing ball. I figured I'd eat my fish sticks fast and join them.

"Hey, snowbird." I looked up and found Billy Peebles leaning over the table toward me. Billy was the biggest kid in our grade, a conch and a bully. He had red hair and freckles and always wore a denim vest with a pack of Now & Laters bulging in the pocket. Three of his friends were with him, and they all wore denim vests too.

"Heard your old man found some silver," Billy said. His father owned Peebles Marine Salvage, the biggest salvage and dredge operation in the lower Keys, and you could count on Billy to know about almost everything that happened offshore.

"That's right," I said.

"What makes him think he can just come down here and take our treasure?" Billy asked, trying to sound ominous.

"It's not yours," I said. "It belongs to whoever finds it."

Billy wasn't real big on intellectual arguments. "This is what I think of snowbirds," he said, leaning over my tray and letting a thick drop of spit fall on my fish sticks. His friends laughed. Mr. Carroll, on lunch duty, was standing only a few feet away. I knew he'd seen everything, but he ignored it.

"Hey, Mr. Carroll, look!" I called as I picked up the plate of fish sticks and squashed it against Billy's chest, smearing his denim vest with fish sticks, grease, and his own spit. Before Billy could take a swing at me, Mr. Carroll grabbed me by the collar and dragged me down to the office.

I got off with a strict warning from Mrs. Wagner, the principal, not to engage in food fights again. I probably would have gotten detention, except that she believed what I told her about Billy spitting on my lunch and Mr. Carroll ignoring it. It was like Tom said—you didn't have to live in Key West long to realize there was a bias against strangers.

At the end of Caroline Street was the shrimp basin, where the shrimp trawlers tied up and unloaded their catches. The shrimpers always picked up crabs and junk fish in their nets, and they tended to dump this stuff in the basin. Over the years bait fish had learned to hang around the basin for easy meals, and they in turn attracted larger fish like barracuda, tarpon, and sharks. Everyone knew the big fish were there, but nobody bothered with them. If a fisherman hired a guide at $300 a day, he wanted to go out in the Gulf, not sit in the basin surrounded by smelly old shrimp boats and staring at the smokestacks of Key West Electric.

In Shannon's skiff I bolted the Penn deep-sea reel to Dad's fishing gaff and lashed the gaff across the oarlocks. The tide was going out, so I ran the skiff to the mouth of the basin. There I sank a shark hook into a tuna head I'd gotten from a cook at the Fisherman's Cafe and ran the line out through a cleat at the bow. My plan was to hook a shark and then use the outboard to tow it into the shallow part of the basin, where it could thrash itself into exhaustion. I wasn't interested in the thrill of landing it with a rod. All I wanted were the teeth.

But first I needed a shark.

The sun was still high overhead, turning the afternoon pleasant and warm. I took off my shirt, leaned back on the boat seat, and let my feet dangle over the side. There was hardly any wind and the water was calm. A couple of brown pelicans sat on wooden pilings watching me, and a dog walked along the railing of one of the shrimp boats watching them. Some gulls glided way above me, and I wondered if they really bombed people on purpose. There was a big debate at school over this. Some kids insisted gulls knew exactly what they were doing when they got you. I tended to think it was accidental—just nature's way of reminding us to wear hats.

I'd gotten a bucket of fish and chicken guts from the Fisherman's Cafe and periodically threw a scoop overboard, hoping it would attract a shark. Like most chum, it smelled terrible and made me think of Billy Peebles. Why should he care if my father found some treasure? Why should anyone? The treasure had always been there. My father had found it because he'd worked hard.

I threw another scoop of chum overboard and watched it splatter on the flat green surface of the water. A lone sea gull dive-bombed a choice morsel and flapped away. I figured a large shark might have forty good-sized teeth, and at $3 each that amounted to $120. If I could catch one a week, I'd give $90 to Mom, $10 to Shannon for the use of her skiff, and keep the rest for myself.

I was just about to toss out another scoop of chum when line started to run off the reel. Keeping my thumb on the spool so it didn't race and get jammed, I waited until the shark had time to swallow the bait. Then I snapped the drag lever closed. The boat lurched as the line went tight and the shark realized it was hooked. The bow slowly turned and began to move out toward the Gulf. From the slow pace I knew the shark wasn't very big. I just hoped its teeth were.

The shark towed me about fifty yards out of the shrimp basin. Then I started the outboard and put it in reverse. The skiff started to back up, the bow dipping and bouncing as the shark fought against the line. There was no way it could win against the outboard, and after about fifteen minutes the bow was hardly bouncing at all. I shut down the outboard and started to crank the reel.

The shark came in easily, and I had a premonition that it was going to be too small. Finally the wire leader came out of the water. I went up to the bow and looked. About four feet under the surface was a five-foot gray shark. I was disappointed and even a little amazed that it had managed to swallow the whole tuna head. From hanging around the fishing docks I'd seen enough sharks to know that this one's teeth weren't nearly big enough. And now I had a new problem. The shark might have been small by shark standards, but it was still a lot bigger than anything I'd caught in the past. Captain Bob carried a rifle on his boat and always killed a shark with a bullet in the brain before it could start thrashing around, destroying equipment and taking bites out of fishermen's legs.

In the water beneath me, the shark jerked its head back and forth, still trying to throw the hook. I reached down and grabbed the wire leader, hoping to pull it out of the water and let it suffocate.

Wham! Something hit the starboard side of the skiff like a torpedo, and I was thrown headfirst into the water. Kicking back to the surface, I heard a high-pitched whining sound, almost like a dentist's drill. At first I thought another boat must've hit Shannon's skiff, but no other boat was around. Next I realized the skiff was starting to move. I managed to grab the gunwale before it got past me. Now whatever was pulling the skiff was pulling me too. But why was the boat moving? What was that sound? And what had knocked me into the water?

The answer raced into my mind just like the yellow blur of the bull shark had raced after my permit the day Tom first took Dad and me fishing. In a flash I worked my way down to the stern, grabbed onto the transom, and hauled myself up. Kicking and twisting, I managed to clamber halfway into the boat. My ribs and stomach got pinched and scratched between the outboard and the transom. My elbows hit the floor and my head banged into the gas can. But at least I'd gotten out of the water. The tops of my thighs were resting against the transom and my feet were where my head should've been. If anyone had been watching from another boat, all they would have seen were two legs sticking in the air.

I stayed like that for a moment, inhaling gasoline vapors as I tried to catch my breath. My ribs and stomach burned where they'd been scraped. The reel was still screaming as line was stripped off, and I could hear water sloshing against the hull as the boat slowly moved ahead. I knew what had happened. Something huge had eaten my shark, something that considered a five-foot gray shark bait.

My first impulse was to cut the line and go home. But the heavy monofilament on the reel was brand-new, and if I cut it, I'd lose more than three hundred yards and Dad would have a fit. Besides, I was in the boat, I had the outboard, I was only a couple of hundred yards offshore. I decided to tighten the drag and see what happened.

The tighter I made the drag, the faster the boat went. Finally the line stopped going out altogether. The boat was being pulled steadily through the water using a new form of energy: fish power.

So there I was, just past my thirteenth birthday, being pulled into the Gulf of Mexico by some underwater monster. My mouth was dry and my heart was banging. I was scared, but excited too. It was around 5:30 in the afternoon, which meant there were at least two hours of sunlight left. Behind me, Key West looked green and tropical. I figured we were headed northwest.

The surest way to lose a big fish is to have too much line out, so I started the outboard and began to catch up, steering with one hand and cranking the reel with the other. It took a while, but I finally recovered about two hundred yards of monofilament. That left about a hundred yards between me and the fish, which was about as close as I wanted to come. I figured Dad would be one third as angry if I lost a hundred yards as if I lost 300 yards.

I guess I didn't realize how fast the fish was mov-

ing, because when I looked back I had a shock. Key
West had become a speck barely visible on the horizon. I couldn't believe how far away it looked. Suddenly I was alone in the Gulf, looking at steel-blue
water in every direction. My stomach started to
churn and I felt my heart beat even harder. Forget
this fish, I thought, pulling out my knife to cut the
line.

Before I could reach the reel the bow suddenly
dipped hard, as if a giant had pulled down on it. The
knife flew out of my hand and over the seat in front of
me, landing on the floor with a clunk. The bow
lurched again and I had to grab the gunwales to
balance myself. The fish was yanking down, as if it
were trying to drag the boat under. I made a grab for
the knife but missed as we lurched again and pulled
hard to the port side. It was like riding a wild bull in
the rodeo.

The skiff danced in the water like a bobber. My
heart was beating so hard, I thought it would burst.
Any second now I expected some huge sea creature
to surface and attack.

Meanwhile, the line grew tighter and tighter. *This
is it!* I thought, bracing for it to snap.

The line grew tight but didn't break. Instead the
fish started swimming again. Now I saw that the bolts
holding the reel on the gaff had shaken loose. In my
mind I could see the bolts letting go and the reel
sailing overboard. It was one thing to lose a few hun-

dred yards of monofilament but another to lose the whole reel. I quickly started the engine and began following the fish, hoping to take the strain off.

The sun was starting to get low. Back in Key West tourists would be heading to Mallory Square. A frigate bird glided overhead, and a big sea turtle came up about thirty feet away and studied me. Life would've been idyllic if I hadn't been connected to a huge sea monster below.

The engine sputtered and quit. I yanked on the cord to restart it, but it wouldn't catch. Looking down at the gas tank, I was stunned to see that it was dead empty. I hadn't checked it before leaving the dock. When Shannon said fill it I'd assumed she meant *after* I used it.

Wham! The bolts let go and the reel shot off the gaff. *Bang!* It hit the inside of the hull and rode up the side. I was certain it was going over, but at the last moment it got caught in a cleat. The boat lurched forward. Once again the fish was pulling me.

No matter how I tried, I couldn't separate myself from the creature below. Behind us Key West had disappeared, leaving nothing except water and sky. It must have been around dinnertime. By now my parents would have noticed my absence. Chances were they'd talk to Betty or Shannon and find out I'd borrowed the skiff. They'd call out the Coast Guard and I'd probably get arrested for all kinds of things.

Meanwhile, the sun was getting lower, and I was on my way to Texas.

A few minutes later the boat stopped. I held on to the gunwales, expecting another bucking bronco ride, but nothing happened. After a while I inched forward and touched the line. It gave under my finger. The fish was gone. Just like that. Vanished. Suddenly I felt depressed. To go through all that and lose the darn fish wasn't right. But I felt relieved too. The skiff had oars.

It was getting dark. A pastel sunset had faded. Venus glowed like a giant star in the west and the North Star sparkled in the sky. The Gulf turned black except for an occasional patch of golden-brown sargasso weed. I put the oars in the oarlocks and started to row.

It was a beautiful, calm evening. As the sky grew darker it filled with stars and a crescent moon. I rowed steadily, listening to the dip of the oars in the water and the creaking of the oarlocks. Soon Venus was no longer visible, but by then I could make out the faint glow of Key West in the southeast. I kept rowing, preoccupied with the excuses and explanations I knew I'd soon have to give.

It must have been an hour or two later that a beam of light threw a shadow on the water behind me. I turned and squinted into a spotlight, just able to make out the trawl booms of a shrimper out for its nightly run. A few minutes later the trawler cut its engines and drifted beside me. Three men stood at the rail next to the wheelhouse.

"Y'all the Cooper boy?" the captain asked with a deep Louisiana accent.

"Yes."

"Wanna come on board?"

"Thanks," I said. "But I think I'll make it back okay."

"Well, then I'll just radio in and give 'em your loran coordinates if you don't mind," the captain said with a chuckle. "I hear there's some folks been lookin' for you."

"Thanks," I said, and started to row again.

I don't think ten minutes passed before I heard the wail of an outboard engine. I looked around and saw another spotlight. A few moments later Tom and Dad came alongside in Tom's boat. In the dark they almost looked like twins, with their wild hair and beards.

Dad grabbed the gunwale of the skiff. I can't repeat what he said, but mixed in with all the swear words was the fact that he was glad I was safe. Tom stood in the dark with his hands on his hips, swaying with the soft rolls of the waves. I could see him scowling at the reel jammed at the bow of the skiff. "What were you doing, Chris?"

"It's too hard to explain," I said.

"I think you better try," said Dad.

"Betty said she needed shark's teeth, and I figured we could use the money," I explained.

I'm not sure Dad heard me. He'd started to pull the monofilament by hand. "Tom," he said, "shine that spotlight over here."

Tom aimed the spotlight at the skiff's bow. From the way Dad was pulling the line I realized something was still attached to it. Soon a dark shadow appeared deep in the water, revolving slowly. Dad gave another pull and all three of us jumped at the same time. We were looking into the face of a huge shark! I felt goose bumps run down my arms and legs and heard Dad catch his breath. A second later he sighed as we saw that it was just the head. The body was gone. Dad started uttering unmentionable things again and Tom added a few of his own. The shark's head was covered with ragged gashes and bites. Even though it was dead, it was still frightening. The mouth was huge, like the opening of a garbage can lined with jagged, pointy teeth. I couldn't believe that I'd actually hooked something so big. *What if it had attacked the boat?* I didn't want to think about it.

Dad stared at me, but before he could begin his lecture I said, "Don't bother. I absolutely, totally swear I'll never do anything like this again. Just don't tell Mom, okay?"

He didn't answer. He just looked down again at the shark's head. There was no way any of us were going to touch it. I could imagine the jaws snapping shut in some weird primal reflex. Finally Tom gaffed it through the snout, and he and Dad hauled it on board. They guessed it was a great white shark and must've weighed a couple of thousand pounds.

We cruised home through the dark, watching the flying fish skim the surface, leaving trails of sparkling phosphorescence. Dad put his arm around my shoulders. I think he was a little amazed that I'd gone out on my own, hooked that shark, and followed it all the way out into the Gulf.

"Well, Chris," he said, "I guess I'd better teach you to dive. It may be the only way to keep you out of trouble."

8

Tom kept the shark's head in his fish freezer overnight, and the next day after school we pulled the
teeth out. I got forty-three big teeth and sold them to
Betty for a grand total of $129. I think she was sur-
prised I'd actually come up with so many. After giv-

ing $10 to Shannon and keeping $10 for myself, I gave the rest to Dad to repair the reel and buy something for Mom.

Two mornings later I was locking my bike to the rack at school when I sensed someone behind me. I turned and found Billy Peebles and some other kids, most of them conchs. One was David Lester, a real handsome kid with black hair and deep blue eyes. The girls were all crazy about him.

"What's this crap about you catching a big shark?" Billy asked.

"I don't know," I answered with a shrug.

"Well, did you or didn't you?"

"I don't have to tell you," I said.

Billy looked perplexed. I guess he figured it was a story I'd made up to make myself look like a hero.

"I heard the head was in Tom Gordon's fish freezer," David Lester said.

"Okay," Billy said. "I'm gonna check it out after school. If it isn't true, you're in trouble."

I didn't think much of it until the next day. We were playing softball in PE and my team was up. David Lester was playing third base. I hit a double and then stretched it into a triple when the left fielder threw the ball over the second baseman's head. As the next kid got up to bat I took a short lead off third. David crouched near the bag.

"How come you told Billy you didn't know anything about that shark?" he asked.

"Wasn't any of his business."

I could see that David couldn't figure this out. In his world any kid who caught a shark that big would want to brag about it to everyone. I stretched my lead a little. David moved closer to the bag in case the pitcher tried to pick me off.

"What'd you want with a shark anyway?" he asked.

"The teeth."

David straightened up and put his hands on his hips. "You weird or something?"

Just then the batter hit a grounder up the third-base line. If David had been ready, he probably would have gotten it, but he was standing there staring at me and the ball went right past him.

"Hey, Lester! Wake up!" the pitcher shouted.

David looked mad. I winked at him and then ran to home plate.

As soon as school let out that summer I started diving full-time with Dad. Shannon came out a lot too. She already knew how to dive and had her own wet suit. Dad said every extra pair of eyes increased the chance of finding treasure.

For weeks we dived near the spot where Dad had found the silver coins, working our way out from it in concentric circles, marking our progress on an oceanographic chart taped inside the cabin of the *Treasure Hunter*. Each time we found something interesting, like an old ballast stone or some broken porcelain plates, we'd mark it on the chart.

"We're looking for a scatter pattern," Dad said during lunch one day. He pointed to a long red line on the chart. "Here's the reef line. The galleon would be driven off course by a hurricane from the south, and the reef would tear a hole in her hull. But she wouldn't sink right away. Instead, the wind and waves would push her along, sometimes for more than a mile, with people and cargo spilling out like groceries out of a torn shopping bag."

We were anchored over a spot that had tripped the magnetometer, and after lunch we got ready to dive again. Because gold and silver were heavy, they usually settled into the sand wherever they fell. Over the centuries the sands shifted and the treasure gradually sank to the bedrock below. In some parts of the Gulf the sand was only a foot or two deep, but in other places it might be ten or fifteen feet deep. We couldn't dig that much sand away by hand, but treasure hunters had invented other ways.

Dad used two big ducts bent into right angles. Each duct was about the diameter of a large garbage pail. One end fit over the *Treasure Hunter*'s props and the other end was aimed down at the sea bottom. When Dad turned on the engines the props would drive a column of water through the ducts and down toward the bottom, where it would blow a hole through the sand right down to the bedrock, leaving a crater ten to twenty feet wide on the ocean floor.

Dad started the *Treasure Hunter*'s engines, and the ducts began to blow holes in the sandy bottom forty feet below. As we strapped on our tanks, we noticed a thick slab of gray clouds blowing in from the southwest.

"Squall coming up," Dad said, nodding his head to the southwest. Afternoon squalls were nothing new. Sometimes, if they weren't too bad, we worked right through them. Other times, we'd anchor the *Treasure Hunter* securely and ride them out.

Shannon and I went over the side. The water was cloudy with sand blown around by the ducts, and small fish darted about gobbling the worms and crabs that were being unearthed. The sand was probably the worst part of diving. It got into our diving gloves, our flippers, even inside our wet suits, where it rubbed against our skin like sandpaper. But bad as it got, the excitement of searching for treasure was always greater.

I followed Shannon down. She always dived with her long blond hair streaming out behind her like a mermaid. On the bottom we were careful not to get too close to the prop wash from the ducts. I'd already gotten caught in it once that summer and had been slammed down onto the bedrock.

As the sand was blown away nothing of interest appeared. I was just about to return to the surface when Shannon swam over and tapped my arm. I quickly saw what had intrigued her. A thick, rusted bar of iron, perhaps five inches long, was sticking out from the sand. I reached down and grabbed it but it wouldn't budge. As the ducts kept blowing the sand away, the iron bar grew before our eyes. Soon a huge iron ring became visible. The shaft connected to the ring was twice as thick as the bar Shannon had found. We watched the shaft grow longer and longer as more sand was washed away. Suddenly, six feet to the right, something dark appeared in the sand, gradually turning into a triangle. That's when I realized what we'd found and raced to the surface.

"An anchor!" I shouted, pulling my mask off. "A huge one!"

Dad's head appeared over the gunwale, a big grin on his face. "I'll be right there," he shouted.

I swam back down. By now most of the anchor was visible. It was gigantic, probably fifteen feet long and twelve feet wide, shaped like two huge *J*'s pressed back-to-back.

Above us Dad plunged into the water. He swam straight to the anchor and began to run his hand up and down the shaft. The entire anchor was now visible and the ducts from the *Treasure Hunter* were still blowing out the crater. Dad gave me the thumbs-up sign.

On the other side of the crater Shannon lifted something from the ocean floor. At first it looked like a piece of old pipe, but then I realized it was a musket whose stock and wood had been eaten away by worms. There must have been two dozen more lying like matchsticks on the rocks beneath her. A whole boxful must have fallen out of the galleon. Dad raced past me to have a look. I knew what he was thinking: If we'd found an anchor and muskets, the treasure couldn't be far away.

Just then I felt the water change. One moment Dad was floating five feet away from me, the next moment he was slammed down against the bottom of the crater. Somehow he'd gotten caught in the prop wash.

Both Shannon and I swam to him. I pressed my thumb and forefinger together making a circle, our sign language for "Are you okay?" Dad nodded back but then pointed upward. I looked up and was amazed to see that the surface was churning. The bottom of the *Treasure Hunter*'s hull was rising and falling wildly in the waves. When the boat tipped up, the angle of the prop wash changed just enough to catch Dad. In our excitement we'd forgotten about the squall. Forty feet below the surface, we'd been completely unaware of the wind and rainstorm raging above.

Dad quickly motioned us to swim up. The *Treasure Hunter*'s engines were running near full throttle. If either of the ducts was knocked off by a wave, she would sail away and leave us stranded in the middle of the sea.

About ten feet from the surface we began to feel the turbulence of the water above. The *Treasure Hunter*'s hull slapped and crashed in the waves, and the rope ladder flapped at her side. Trying to board the boat would be dangerous. We had to avoid getting hit by the hull or swept into the spinning drive shafts that turned the propellers. But there was no choice. Someone had to get into the boat and stop the engines.

Fighting the waves and turbulence, Dad swam to the surface. Each time the hull fell he grabbed for the rope ladder, but in the meantime he was getting battered by the waves. Once he nearly got swept under, and the hull grazed his shoulder. Finally he managed to grab the bottom rung. Kicking his fins off, he started to climb up. Shannon swam after the loose fins. I waved to her not to bother, but she didn't see me.

Dad hauled himself into the boat, and a few seconds later the propellers stopped turning. Shannon was about fifteen feet away, swimming back with Dad's fins. A life ring hit the surface above me, and I reached for it and let Dad pull me toward the ladder. I grabbed the lowest rung and managed to hang on until Dad pulled me in.

The deck was slick with rainwater. Big drops pelted us as I held on to the cabin door for balance while Dad stripped off my tank and weight belt. By now Shannon should have been alongside the boat. I looked over the side, but she wasn't there. The choppy water made it difficult to see beneath the surface, but I knew something was wrong. Grabbing the life ring, I vaulted back over the side into the crashing waves.

As soon as I was underwater I saw Shannon trapped under the boat, her long blond hair caught in the port drive shaft. Even though the shaft wasn't turning, her hair had gotten tangled around it in the turbulent water and she was trying to pull it free. Just then the hull rose on a wave and crashed down hard on her head. I swear I heard the *bonk!* as the hull hit her. Shannon went limp and the bubbling mouthpiece fell from her lips.

I swam to her. Almost out of breath myself, I grabbed her mouthpiece, stuck it in my mouth, and took a big breath, then pushed it back between her lips. I grabbed her hair and tried to pull it free, but it wouldn't give. The hull rose and crashed down again, nearly hitting us. Shannon was still limp. There was only one thing to do. I reached for the diving knife I kept in a sheath on my right leg.

A moment later we broke through the churning waves about five feet from the boat. Shannon was still out of it. I wound the life ring under her arms and Dad pulled her in. I climbed the rope ladder. It was a lot easier this time without the tank and weight belt.

On deck, Dad had Shannon doubled over at the waist and was slapping her on the back. I heard her gag, cough, and gasp for breath. Luckily for us, the squall was brief. Already the waves were starting to lose their force, and the boat was no longer rocking so furiously. I realized I was shaking all over. Shannon started to cry, and Dad sat on the deck and held her, telling her she was okay. What was left of her long blond hair looked like it had been chewed up in a lawn mower. Dad and I glanced at each other. I knew he must have been angry at the risk I'd taken, but I think he was surprised too. I know I was.

9

After the squall passed Dad made one more dive to
attach a Clorox-bottle buoy to the anchor so we could
find it again. He also brought the muskets up. Shannon sat in the cabin wrapped in a blanket, her eyes
red and her nose running. You'd imagine that after

surviving a scare like that, we'd all be happy, but we weren't. Hardly a word was spoken. Each of us seemed to prefer being alone with his thoughts.

On deck, the muskets looked more like ornaments than actual firearms, their matchlocks and barrels etched with flowery designs. We studied them for a few moments and then Dad said we were going home.

The sun came out and the wind died down. Shannon changed into a sweatshirt and cutoffs and sat on the forward deck. She pulled what was left of her hair over her shoulder and tried to braid it. All the severed, uneven ends had dried stiffly, making her look like a punk rocker.

In the cabin Dad sat behind the wheel, steering with one hand and drinking a Coke. The *Treasure Hunter*'s old diesel engines grumbled beneath us, and a slight scent of exhaust seeped up through the floor.

"You did a brave thing," he said. "Just promise me you'll never do it again. You scared the bejesus out of me."

I half nodded.

"If something goes wrong," Dad said, "it's my problem. Let me take care of it, okay?"

"Okay."

"Not a word to your mother, smart guy."

"What about Shannon's hair?" I asked.

The furrows in Dad's forehead deepened and he

ran his fingers through his own tangled hair. "I'll think of something."

Up on the deck, Shannon glanced back at us.

"Why don't you go talk to her," Dad said.

"You think she wants me to?"

Dad shrugged. "You'll find out."

I walked up front holding the rail. The wind was in my face, and the sun had turned the water a murky green. As we crashed over the small waves, flying fish shot out to the right and left, skimming the water for forty or fifty feet and then plunging back in again. A mottled gray-green porpoise swam in front of the bow, probably thinking we were a fishing boat and hoping for some unused bait. Shannon sat hunched forward into the wind, her knees tucked up under her chin, the end of her braid clenched tightly in her hand.

"You okay?" I asked, sitting down next to her.

She nodded and glanced at the braid in her hand.

"It'll grow back," I said, hoping she'd find such an obvious statement funny.

"It's not that," she said.

"Then what is it?"

"My head hurts," she said, rubbing the spot where the hull had hit her. "It was scary getting caught under there. Thanks for saving me."

"No sweat," I said. "Next time you can save me."

* * *

We dropped Shannon off at her house and went next door to ours. Mom came out of the bedroom wearing her waitressing outfit.

"Home early today," she said, giving us a curious look.

Dad and I were caught off guard. We were so used to coming home after she'd left for work.

"Uh, made a big find," Dad announced, trying to sound excited.

"Treasure?" Mom brightened.

"Well, no, an anchor and some muskets," Dad said. "But it's a good sign."

Mom rolled her eyes. Obviously she didn't see what was so good about it. She picked up her bag and checked her hair one last time.

"So, uh, how's it going?" Dad asked.

"What? At the Pier House?" Mom looked at him incredulously. She was starting her second year as a waitress. These days it was just a matter of bringing home a check.

"Hon, it's only till I find the treasure," Dad said, trying to soothe her.

"Don't." Mom raised her hands to her ears as if she couldn't stand listening to his promises anymore. I realized why I often felt weird and guilty around her. Dad and I loved what we were doing, but every day we let her go off to do something she hated.

* * *

The next six weeks of diving were the most productive ever. Drawing lines through the anchor and the spot where he'd found the silver coins, Dad created a rough scatter pattern, and almost every day we found a new artifact—a stone cannonball, some copper plates, a long, pointed spearhead, some spoons and knives.

Once word got out that we were finding relics, people started coming down to the docks each evening to see what we'd brought up that day. Some even asked if they could dive with us, but Dad was wary of strangers and always said no. One night, though, we came in late because Dad had trouble with the *Treasure Hunter*'s engines. It was dark, but a lone figure was waiting next to our slip. He was a square-jawed muscular guy with short sandy hair, wearing a white T-shirt, cutoff sweatpants, and basketball high tops. Sort of looked like a football player in training camp. From the paleness of his skin, I knew he'd just arrived in town.

"Sorry, didn't find anything today," Dad said as he hopped up on the dock and threw a rope around a cleat.

"That's okay, Mr. Cooper," the guy said, stepping closer. "You are Mr. Cooper, aren't you?"

Dad nodded and jumped back down into the *Treasure Hunter*.

"My name's Bobby Clark," the guy said. "I just came from St. Louis, Missouri, to dive with you."

Dad picked up our Styrofoam cooler. While waiting for him to fix the engines, Shannon and I'd caught a bunch of snappers, and the cooler was full of fish and ice. It must've weighed a ton. Dad heaved it up on the gunwale. "Well, uh, I appreciate that, Bobby, but to be honest, I've got all the divers I need."

"Then maybe I can help on the boat," Bobby said eagerly.

"Sorry, but I don't think so," Dad said. I could see him strain to lift the cooler to the dock.

"Let me give you a hand," Bobby said. He reached down, took the cooler with practically no effort, and placed it gently on the dock.

"Uh, thanks." Dad seemed a little astonished.

"You sure there isn't some way I can help out?" Bobby asked.

Something about him must have gotten to Dad. Maybe it was his eagerness, or his strength, or both. The next thing I knew, Dad said, "Well, I wouldn't be able to pay you."

"That's okay," Bobby said with a smile.

"And if we find any treasure, it's got to go toward paying off debts before I can give out any shares," Dad said.

"That's okay too," said Bobby.

"Can't even give you a place to live," Dad said.

"Maybe I could stay here and keep an eye on your boat," Bobby said.

Shannon—who had a new, short haircut—and I

glanced at each other. Live on the boat? I think we were both surprised when Dad said, "Okay."

The next morning I half expected to find Bobby and the *Treasure Hunter* gone. But as we rode up to the dock on our bikes, Bobby came out of the cabin carrying two air tanks in each hand. The muscles in his arms bulged. Out on the deck he started the air compressor and began filling the tanks.

"Where'd you learn that?" Dad asked as he got off his bike.

"A dive shop in St. Louis," Bobby replied.

"Where do you dive in St. Louis?" Shannon asked with a scowl.

Bobby grinned. "Pools, mostly."

As we sailed out toward the treasure site Bobby told us he was a sophomore in college and worked at the dive shop every summer. Earlier in the week one of the regular customers had come in and said he'd been down in Key West and had seen some of the artifacts Dad had brought up.

"I left the next morning," Bobby said.

"Just like that?" Dad asked.

"I know it sounds crazy," Bobby said. "But this is what I've dreamed about my whole life."

About an hour later we anchored over the scatter pattern. Dad put down the ducts and started blasting craters in the sand about fifty feet below. Bobby and I dived first. At fifty feet the water starts to filter out certain colors. Blues and greens get washed out and yellow is barely discernible. We swam around the crater for a while and didn't see anything. Bobby picked up something small and slipped it into his wet suit, but I figured he was just collecting souvenirs. Dad blasted another crater, and we didn't find anything there either. It looked like it was going to be a quiet morning.

After a while we ran out of air and returned to the boat.

"I hate to say it," Dad said as he helped Bobby pull off his tank and weight belt, "but this is what it's like most of the time. You look in a lot of empty holes."

"That's cool," Bobby said. "Besides, I did find a piece of copper." He pulled a small flat bar out of his wet suit. It was dented and notched, about six inches long and a quarter of an inch thick.

Dad gasped. Bobby's eyes looked like they were going to pop out of their sockets. The bar may have looked dark and coppery at fifty feet, but in the sunlight it glistened the way only gold can.

"I don't believe it!" Bobby cried. Shannon and I crowded around as Dad inspected the bar.

"See the double X stamped in the metal?" he said excitedly. "That means it's twenty karat. These curving letters are the royal tax stamp. This is it! This is real Spanish treasure!"

We heard a splash and looked up just in time to see Bobby's flippers as he swam back down to the bottom. He was wasting no time looking for more treasure. Dad rubbed the gold bar between his fingers and smiled. "I had a feeling he'd bring us luck."

By the end of the afternoon we'd found some gold coins and a dented gold cup with winged mermaids engraved in the rim. Seeing the treasure was the greatest feeling in the world. Dad was grinning from ear to ear. Once again he'd proved the skeptics wrong.

That night we had a party. After two years in Key West we knew more people than could fit in our house, and the crowd spilled out into the street, talking loudly at the curb and under the streetlight. Back inside, Dad lay the gold out on the kitchen table for everyone to see. Mom was a little nervous about leaving it out in plain sight, but Dad just hugged her and said, "Don't worry, hon, there's plenty more where this came from."

Outside, Shannon and I sat at the curb drinking pop and feeling giddy about the day's finds. We were trying to decide what we'd do when we were all rich.

"I'm gonna get a fifty-foot Hatteras Sportfisherman," I said, "tournament-rigged, with a tuna tower, Pompanette fighting chairs, and all custom-built rods. And I'm gonna fish a whole year and see how many world records I can break."

"I'd have to give some to charity," Shannon said. "Then I'd put some away for college and my trawler.

And then I'd go to the best restaurant in Miami and order the biggest steak they had."

"What would your mom say?" I asked.

"She'd understand."

I was just about to tell her I'd join her for the steak when Billy Peebles, David Lester, and some other kids came by on bikes. Instead of joining the party, they rode around under a nearby streetlight, watching the festivities.

"Friends?" Dad asked me.

"Not exactly," I said.

Dad glanced at them again. "Maybe they'd like some pop."

I got the message and went inside and got a bottle of Dr Pepper and some cups. Back outside, Billy stopped riding and eyed Shannon and me suspiciously.

"Want some pop?" I asked.

It was funny how Billy's friends looked at him first, as if they needed his okay. Only David Lester seemed to have a mind of his own. "Sure, thanks," he said.

I poured him a cup and one for Shannon and me. The others watched.

"You can see what we found if you want," I said. "It's back in the house."

They didn't seem to know what to do and kept watching Billy. Finally he stopped riding and said he wanted some pop. I gave him a cup and he started to drink it. Suddenly he sneezed and pop dripped out of his nose. As his friends laughed he tugged the sleeve of his T-shirt under his nose and wiped it. Shannon looked disgusted. I had a feeling it was a stunt he'd pulled before.

"Aw, shucks," Billy said in mock apology. "I'm so sorry. Hope I didn't ruin your little party."

He and his friends rode away into the dark, laughing.

Most of the people at the party had no idea what had happened, and I wasn't about to tell them. Shannon and I sat down on the curb again, a little way from the celebration. The moon was almost full, and up in the sky over Cudjoe Key we could see Fat Albert, the big white radar blimp the government used to detect low-flying drug planes.

"Billy Peebles is without a doubt the dumbest person in Key West," Shannon said.

I guess I was supposed to laugh, but I didn't. Billy wasn't a genius, but he wasn't totally dumb either. It was depressing. I'd never given him a reason to hate me.

"You know," I said, "it's kind of funny, how no matter how dumb or prejudiced someone may be, you'd still be happier if they liked you."

"They used to make fun of my mom," Shannon said, gazing up at the moon. "The kids heard she meditated and was a vegetarian. At school a couple of times they made me cry. Mom said if I ignored them, they'd stop teasing me because it's no fun to tease someone who doesn't react. So that's what I did and it worked."

"If you ignore them, they think you're a snob," I said.

"I didn't ignore them all the time," Shannon said. "Just when they started to tease."

I wasn't convinced. It couldn't hurt to try, but Billy Peebles didn't seem like the kind of person who was easy to ignore.

The party continued in front of our house, but Shannon and I sat quietly on the curb, watching the occasional lizard or palmetto bug wander by. I just couldn't get Billy off my mind.

"I mean, what does he want?" I asked. "Is he jealous? Hey, maybe that's it! Maybe he's got a secret crush on you!"

"Billy?" Shannon looked at me like I was crazy.

"I'm serious!"

"No way! I wouldn't wish that on my worst enemy."

We were having a few laughs speculating on Billy Peebles's secret love life when I heard the scratch of tires on the sandy street. David Lester had come back, alone.

"Could I see it?" he asked.

I couldn't help smiling. "Sure."

Shannon and I led him into the kitchen and showed him the gold bar, coins, and dented cup lying on the table along with bottles of pop and bags of Cheetos. David bent down for a better look.

"Here." I picked up the gold bar and handed it to him.

He looked surprised that we'd let him touch it. Like most of us, he was unprepared for how heavy even a small bar of pure gold felt. He balanced it in his hand and ran his fingers along its uneven edge. "How'd you find it?"

I explained about the scatter pattern and how we blew craters in the sand with the prop ducts.

"So it took two years?" he asked, gazing down at the other pieces of treasure on the table.

"But this is just the beginning," I said. "There should be a lot more."

David looked around the Shack. Mom had never been real interested in fixing it up, so the walls were still bare and some of the window shades were ripped. I'd heard that David lived in a big old conch house that had been in his family for generations. His father owned Lester's Boat Yard, the biggest in Key West, and David had his own jet ski and a Donzi speedboat.

"How long do you think it'll take to find the rest of the treasure?" he asked.

"Could be tomorrow, could be ten years," I said.

David nodded. I couldn't tell from his expression if he thought that sounded crazy or made perfect sense. He took one last look around and then handed the gold bar back to me. "Well, thanks," he said. "See ya around."

Shannon and I watched him go out the screen door.

"What was that all about?" I asked.

She shrugged. "With conchs you never know."

The next morning Dad took the treasure up to Miami. Four days later he returned with all kinds of things—a dress for Mom, a new wet suit for me, and a State of Florida Admiralty Injunction that gave him the exclusive right to search for treasure in the scatter pattern.

But his most interesting acquisition arrived a week later. The *Dolphin* was a sixty-five-foot Coast Guard cutter he'd bought at auction in Fort Lauderdale.

"Wait till you see her props," Dad said when he took Mom, Shannon, and me down to the city marina. "They're huge. We'll dig craters four times the size of the ones we get now."

Everything Dad told us about the *Dolphin* sounded great. It slept ten and had a working galley. It was big enough to withstand almost any kind of weather. We could anchor it permanently over the treasure site and keep teams of divers going from morning until night. As we rode down North Roosevelt Avenue I imagined a long, sleek modern ship painted Coast Guard white.

A few minutes later we stood on the dock staring at

a rusty gray hulk riddled with bullet holes. She was definitely a cutter, with the distinctive raised bow for cutting through rough seas, a midship bridge housing the captain's cabin and navigation room, and a rounded stern. What Dad hadn't told us was that the *Dolphin*'s last official function for the Coast Guard had been target practice.

"You paid money for this?" Mom asked.

"I got a great deal," Dad said.

"I'll bet," she groaned.

On the stern deck a pump spewed water into the marina.

"What's the pump for?" Shannon asked.

"Uh, some of the holes are below the waterline," Dad said.

"You mean if you turn it off, it'll sink?" Mom asked.

Dad slipped his arm around her waist. "Don't worry, hon, in a month it'll be good as new."

10

September came and it was hard to stop diving and go back to school, but when I did I noticed something funny had happened. I was no longer just another "snowbird." Now I was "the treasure hunter's kid." Kids who'd ignored me in the past paid attention.

Some were friendly. Some, like Billy Peebles, were not.

In town it was the same way. Almost seemed as if the population of Key West had divided into two camps—those rooting for us and those against us. Dad said it was best to ignore the whole thing. But it turned out a lot easier to say than do.

One night just after school started, Bobby Clark and I rode down to the shrimp basin, where the *Dolphin* was docked while workmen refitted her for treasure hunting.

It was dark and cloudy, and we couldn't see any stars. To our right the lights from the Navy base sparkled on the black water. To our left were the dark silhouettes of the shrimp trawlers and the *Dolphin*. Some of the trawler cabins were lit, and from one we heard country music playing on a radio. The other sound was the incessant putting of the pump keeping the *Dolphin* afloat.

We sat down on the old wooden pier. I noticed Bobby was wearing one of Betty's shark's teeth on a chain. He pulled one knee up under his chin and let the other leg dangle from the pier. Blond hair corkscrewed off his tanned knees.

"Classes start in three days," he said. "I gotta decide whether to go back."

"Why wouldn't you?" I asked.

"You kidding, Chris?" Bobby looked surprised. "This is the most exciting thing I've ever done. How in the world am I gonna go back and sit in classes all day?"

"I didn't think you had a choice," I said. "I sure don't."

Bobby smiled. "Listen. There's something I gotta ask you. You think your dad's really gonna stick with this thing? I mean, I don't mind skipping a couple of semesters if I know he's in it for the long run. I just don't want to drop out and then discover he's gotten bored and decided to do something else."

"I don't think he can afford to do anything else," I said. Bobby thought about that. I guess he was making his decision about school. After a few moments I said, "Won't your parents be ticked?"

Bobby gazed out at the boats. "It's kind of strange, Chris. See, my mother's blind and my father's been in a wheelchair since he was five years old. I mean, they do almost everything regular people do, but they don't get all hot and bothered about stuff like college. Like, they're just happy me and my brother and two sisters can see and walk. The other thing is, they've never been to the ocean. The idea of diving for treasure is incredible to them. So every week I try to write a letter about what I'm doing down here. My sister says every time they get one of my letters my mom makes my dad read it to her about five times."

I guess my jaw must've dropped, because Bobby looked at me and laughed. "Hey, it's no big deal. I told you, they're just like other people."

"I know, but—" Before I could continue Bobby held up his hand. It seemed like he was listening to something.

"I don't hear it," he said.

"What?"

"The pump."

He was right. The putting sound had stopped and all we could hear was the shrimper's country music. Bobby jumped up, and we ran down the dock to the *Dolphin* and climbed on board. Bobby crouched next to the pump.

"Can't see anything in the dark," he said. "You better go get your dad. I'll try to get the hand crank to work."

"You can't pump this boat by hand," I said.

"I know," Bobby said. "That's why you better get your dad."

I rode home as fast as I could. Sweat dripped down my face and arms in the hot humid air. When I got to the Shack I could see Dad through the window, sitting at the kitchen table working on a regulator from an air tank.

"Dad!" I burst into the house. "The *Dolphin*'s pump stopped!"

He jumped up and ran into the bedroom. A moment later he was back with his toolbox and a flashlight. Outside, he threw them into the basket of his bike and took off. I followed.

At the dock we could see Bobby on the *Dolphin*'s

deck, pumping the hand crank like the jack on a car. The *Dolphin* was already starting to list. We had to get the pump going fast, because the lower she got, the more holes would be below the waterline.

Bobby had pulled off his shirt and his skin glistened with sweat. "She's goin' fast, and this hand crank ain't worth a thing."

"I could've told you that," Dad said, crouching next to the pump. "You check the gas?"

"Yeah, the tank's got plenty."

Dad quickly shone the flashlight over the pump's engine. The dock creaked and groaned as the sinking ship pulled its mooring lines tight. *Pow!* We heard a sound like a gunshot.

"What the . . . ?" Bobby gasped.

"Mooring line snapped!" Dad shouted. He reached under the pump's gas tank. "The feed's disconnected. Get ready to start her, Bobby."

Bobby grabbed the pull cord. Dad was turning something under the gas tank. We were all trying to keep our balance on the slanting deck. The dock creaked louder. *Bang!* Another line exploded.

"Start her!" Dad shouted. Bobby yanked, but the engine didn't catch. He pulled again.

The pump caught, sputtered, and died. *Whap!* Still another line went.

"Get off!" Dad shouted to me as he jumped up and took the pull cord. "You, too, Bobby. Off the dock. If she goes, she could take the whole thing with her."

Bobby and I jumped down to the dock and ran. Behind us we could hear the pilings groan as the *Dolphin* listed. Dad gave the engine another pull and the pump started. Water began splashing into the shrimp basin.

"Come on," I yelled to him.

But Dad didn't follow. He turned the pump up as high as it would go. We could see him silhouetted by the lights from the Navy base, bracing himself against the railing like a captain determined to stay with his ship. The pump engine roared. Seconds passed slowly. The *Dolphin* was still listing, the dock still creaking. Had she already taken too much water?

Bobby and I stood in the dark holding our breath, listening to the pump and the sound of water splashing into the shrimp basin. Dad stayed with his ship. Once again, he amazed me. For most of my life he'd simply been a Spanish teacher. Now he was an adventurer, a treasure hunter, even a hero.

The *Dolphin* slowly began to right itself. Dad turned the pump down to its normal speed and checked the remaining mooring lines. Assured that she'd make it through the night, he jumped onto the dock and joined us.

Later, as we pulled our bikes through the gate, Betty came out of her house wearing a long white robe.

"What's all the commotion?" she asked. "You boys took off before like a couple of jackrabbits."

Dad invited her in and we sat down at the kitchen table, which was still covered with regulator parts. Bobby got a couple of beers out of the refrigerator and Dad told Betty what had happened.

"The bolt holding the gas feed probably just vibrated loose," he said.

"Or it could've been done intentionally," Bobby added.

"One of those shrimpers, I'll bet," Betty said. "They're an ornery bunch. Probably didn't want to listen to that pump all night."

Bobby pressed his lips together. He didn't look convinced.

"You think it's more than that, don't you?" Betty asked.

"Who knows?" Bobby said, taking a sip of his beer. "You know how these conchs feel. We could just as easily be some big developer building a new resort. If we find treasure, it means more treasure hunters, more tourists, more disruptions."

"True," Betty allowed. "But I still doubt anyone would go to such lengths."

"Look," Dad said. "We'll probably never know what happened. The point is, the ocean bottom is public domain. It belongs as much to some cabdriver in Cincinnati as it does to any conch here. I sincerely hope what happened tonight wasn't intentional, but even if it was, it's going to take a lot more than vandalizing a boat to stop us from hunting for that treasure."

Bobby tapped his beer against my father's and winked. "Darn straight, partner."

A month later the *Dolphin* was ready. Bobby had decided not to go back to college, and Dad made him captain. He signed up five other divers as well. They were all in their early twenties, and all agreed to work for room and board in return for a share of the treasure.

Dad kept the *Treasure Hunter* and the *Dolphin* permanently anchored over the treasure site and bought a twenty-five-foot Mako to carry divers and supplies out to them. All of a sudden he had three boats and nine divers, including Shannon and me on the weekends. The treasure operation had gone bigtime.

Money was still a problem. Even though the divers brought up emerald rings, gold chains, and a solid disk of gold, it was difficult to put a price on these treasures and they were hard to sell. Meanwhile, the cost of fuel alone ran into hundreds of dollars a day. We were always trying to find ways to make a few extra bucks.

After the tourist trade, shrimping was Key West's most valuable industry. The tons of shrimp the commercial trawlers netted each week were shipped to markets and restaurants all over the country. The shrimp ran only at night, and if you didn't happen to have a shrimp trawler, you could net them from the old railroad bridge. Shannon said she knew of kids who'd landed $600 worth of jumbo shrimp, some as big as ten inches, in a single night. That kind of money could really help Dad out.

One Friday afternoon I heard that the shrimp were running. Shannon was out tending her stone crab traps, and I waited until she got home.

"Want to go shrimping tonight?" I asked as she rode up on her bike and put the kickstand down.

"Where?"

"Off the railroad bridge."

She looked at me like I was crazy.

"Come on, Shan," I said. "No one owns that bridge. We have just as much right to use it as anyone else."

"That's not what the conchs think," she said. "Spots on that bridge get handed down from generation to generation. People've been shot for using someone else's spot."

"Then let's just go take a look," I said. "I mean, have you ever seen it? Aren't you curious?"

"No."

"Look, just come with me. Okay?"

Shannon sighed. "You know, you're just like your father."

It was cold that night. At least, cold by Key West standards—in the low fifties and windy enough to make the palm fronds rustle noisily. Shannon wore jeans, a heavy sweater, and a down vest. I dressed pretty warmly myself. We rode along A1A in the dark, listening to the wind whistle through the spokes of our bikes. Shannon's hair, which was again shoulder length, danced wildly in the wind. She was quieter than usual.

"How come you're so quiet?" I asked as I pedaled alongside her. "You mad or something?"

Shannon shook her head. "Chris, this is none of my business, but your mom's really unhappy."

"How do you know?" I asked.

"My mom was telling me tonight at dinner."

Actually, I wasn't surprised. Mom and Dad were barely speaking again, and it was hard to remember the last time she'd been in a really good mood. Lately I suspected Dad was purposely avoiding her by not coming home until after she left for work.

"Maybe now that Dad's finding some treasure, she won't have to be a waitress anymore," I said.

"It's not that," Shannon said. "It doesn't matter whether she works or not. She's unhappy because there's nothing here for her. She doesn't have any friends. She talks to my mom sometimes, but they're so different."

"Dad'll do something about it," I said. "He always does." This may have been wishful thinking, but I didn't know what else to say.

* * *

The railroad bridge was already crowded when we got there. Years before it had been paved so that people could fish off it. Coleman lanterns, hibachis, and even a few wood fires crackled in the dark, providing light as people wearing hats and heavy jackets prepared their nets. There were kids, adults, even old people, and you could see that most of them planned to make a night of it. They'd brought folding chairs, blankets, thermoses, and sleeping bags.

Shannon and I parked our bikes and walked onto the bridge. I have to admit I felt a little nervous. In two years in Key West I'd never seen anything like this. It felt like we were sneaking up on a secret tribal ceremony.

Scattered clouds raced past the moon. To the west the cloud line was thicker. Soon the moon would be hidden behind them. I leaned against the rail and looked over the side. Below us the water was black and choppy from the wind. Every few moments a dash of milky moonlight would sparkle on the surface, only to disappear as the next cloud approached.

"Bet you ain't never seen nothin' like this." We turned and found an old woman sitting behind us in a folding chair. She had a plaid blanket on her lap and a red scarf tied over her head. She knew we were strangers.

"Can't say I have," I replied.

"Where're you from?" she asked.

"Well, actually, I've lived here for two years." I pointed at Shannon. "She's lived here for ten."

The old woman nodded and took out a corncob pipe. Shannon and I gaped at each other while she cupped her hands and lit it. Neither of us had ever seen a woman smoke a pipe before.

"Uh, how come no one's started shrimping yet?" I asked.

"Ain't enough tide," the old woman said, puffing. "Just stick around. You'll see."

Shannon and I continued down the bridge. People were cooking hot dogs on hibachis, kids sat on upside-down plastic pails listening to music on boom boxes. Men stood in groups by their nets, talking and watching the dark water as if waiting for a signal that it was time to start.

Shannon said the best shrimping was near the center of the bridge where the channel was the deepest. This was where the oldest conch families would be. We had just reached the middle of the span when someone yelled, "Hey, what are you doing here?" I turned around and saw Billy Peebles coming toward me wearing a big green coat with the hood pulled up. He looked as if he were dressed for a blizzard.

"I asked what you were doing here, rich kid?"

"I'm not a rich kid," I said. Several of Billy's ever-present followers joined him.

"Oh, yeah?" Billy said. "What about the treasure your old man's been finding?"

"He has to sell it to pay for his boats and divers," I said.

"I heard he doesn't even pay his divers," a kid named Dennis said. He had curly brown hair and was the smallest one of the bunch.

"He gives them food and a place to live," I said. "And if they ever hit it big, they'll each get a share."

"I heard he owes a lot of people money," said Billy.

"He'll pay them back," I said.

I could see that Shannon wanted to leave, but Billy and his friends blocked our way. It seemed as if they were trying to think of more antagonistic things to say but couldn't come up with anything good.

Finally Billy said, "I hear your mother's a tramp."

I stared at him in disbelief. "Billy, did anyone ever tell you you have the IQ of a dead starfish?"

A couple of his friends snickered. One of them actually laughed out loud. In the dark I could see Billy's face turn as red as his hair. I had a feeling his embarrassment would quickly turn into fury, so I grabbed Shannon's hand and headed toward Dennis, figuring he'd be the easiest one to push past. Dennis actually jumped out of the way, but before I could get past him, Billy grabbed the collar of my jacket and pulled me backward. I broke my fall with my hands, scraping them on the crumbling pavement of the bridge.

Billy pulled off his coat and crouched over me, his hands in fists. "Come on, big mouth, get up."

I knew there was no way I could outbox him. He was bigger, stronger, and had a longer reach. My one chance was a surprise attack. Pretending to get up slowly, I got to my feet and then charged, trying to butt him in the stomach with my head. I managed to knock him backward and we both went down on the pavement. Almost instantly Billy spun around and twisted my right arm behind my back, pinning me facedown. As my chin scraped against the broken cement, I remembered that Billy wrestled heavyweight for the JV wrestling team.

"Now you're gonna eat dirt, snowbird," he snarled.

"Let him go," another voice said. It sounded like David Lester, but all I could see were tennis shoes.

"Drop dead," Billy said.

"I said let him go."

"Why?"

" 'Cause it's stupid to pick a fight with him. He didn't do anything to you."

"He said I had the IQ of a starfish," Billy whined.

"And you said his mother was a tramp," David replied. "So you're both geniuses."

Billy loosened his grip on my arm. I got up and took my time brushing myself off to show I wasn't scared of him. Both my hands stung from being scraped on the concrete, and my palms had thin red streaks where the skin had been broken. My chin felt raw too. David, wearing a blue parka and a ski cap, was standing near Shannon. I nodded at him as if to say thanks, and he nodded back. Shannon and I started to walk away, but Billy couldn't resist one more insult.

"Hey, is that your hippie girlfriend?" he shouted behind us.

"Just friends," I replied.

His friends laughed, and if Billy said anything more, it was lost in the wind. I turned to Shannon. "Don't let it bother you."

She didn't answer, but as we got to our bikes I heard a sniff and saw her wipe a tear out of her eye.

"What is it?" I asked.

She shook her head. "Nothing."

"Come on, you know Billy's a jerk."

"I know, but I just hate the way you acted."

"Me?" I couldn't believe it. "What did I do?"

"You had to fight with him. You had to make it worse."

"What did you expect me to do? Just let him push us around?"

"I told you the best thing to do is ignore him," Shannon said.

"How was I supposed to ignore him when they had us cornered?" I asked.

Instead of answering, Shannon got on her bike and rode away. I couldn't remember us ever disagreeing before, and for the first time in my life I felt that jumbled-up sensation of liking someone but being mad at them too. Like the way my parents must've felt about each other. Shannon was fifty yards down A1A, riding under the highway lights. Something in my head told me not to catch up.

11

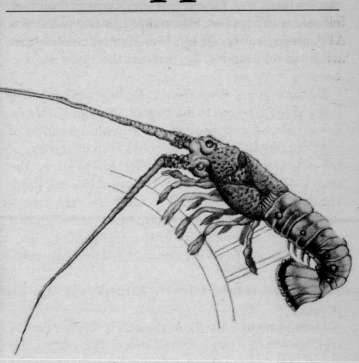

Fall turned to winter, and the scatter pattern began to yield less treasure. Dad kept all the divers working, but I could see that the strain and disappointment were grating on him. He and Mom fought all the time about money. Now that he'd made some, she was mad that he was spending most of it on fuel, repairs, and supplies. She wanted to take what was left and go back north, but Dad kept on insisting that what they'd found so far was just the tip of the iceberg.

By spring the divers were finding nothing, and some of them began to drift away. Dad bought a suit, got a haircut, and headed north with a handful of gold doubloons to see if he could convince some of his old friends around Flintville to invest in the search. Two weeks later he returned looking grim. His suit was wrinkled and I could see dark sweat-stains in the armpits. He dropped his jacket over a chair and took a beer out of the refrigerator.

"How'd it go?" I asked, although it was pretty obvious.

"Not well, Chris. I barely earned back my expenses."

Mom came in from the bedroom. It was her day off and she was in a rare cheerful mood. She smiled and kissed him. Maybe absence really did make the heart grow fonder.

"Let's go out for dinner tonight," she said, trying to cheer him up.

"Don't have any cash," Dad said wearily. "And my credit cards are all overdrawn."

"I've got money," Mom said.

Dad rolled the cold beer can across his forehead, trying to cool himself. He looked at the kitchen clock and blinked. "Darn, I promised Bobby I'd meet him at the boat yard at five to look at that crack in the Mako's hull." He grabbed his jacket and left.

The screen door slapped closed behind him, and the Shack suddenly seemed very quiet. The smile on Mom's face disappeared. "It's hopeless," she said with a shrug, and went back into her room.

By summer we no longer had enough money to keep the boats running all the time. We'd dive for treasure until the gas tanks ran dry, and then we'd trap crawfish and stone crabs until we'd made enough money to buy another fifty-gallon drum of diesel. At night we'd put out shark lines with grouper heads, and in the morning, if we'd caught anything, we'd hack the teeth out and sell them to Betty and the other jewelry-makers.

That fall the *Treasure Hunter* had to go into dry-dock at Lester's Boat Yard until Dad found the money to overhaul her engines. He and Bobby were the only full-time divers left. Shannon and I went to Key West High. We never talked about how we were going to spend our riches anymore. Almost a year had passed since the last piece of eight had been found. Dad needed cash so badly, he finally sold the Penn fishing reel.

One day after school I came home and found Mom sitting on my bed. Usually by the time I got home she'd be dressed in her waitressing outfit, but that day she was wearing jeans. I noticed a suitcase in the kitchen.

"They just called from Flintville," she said. "My mother had a heart attack last night. She's in the hospital."

"Is she okay?" I asked.

"They don't know yet," Mom said. One of her legs was crossed over the other and she was swinging it nervously. "I'm catching the Piedmont flight at four. Betty's going to drive me over to the airport"—she paused and stared down at the floor—"I'm not coming back, Chris."

I looked down at the floor too. I don't think I'd ever noticed how crummy it was. The linoleum had turned yellow and the edges were curled up and chipped. Mom kept swinging her leg. It was weird how neither of us could look at the other. I felt guilty because I'd pretended for so long not to notice how unhappy she'd been. And I guess she felt bad that she was finally giving up.

"You tell Dad?" I asked.

She shook her head. "I can't. This isn't the first time I've decided to leave, Chris. But each time he manages to talk me out of it. You know how persuasive he can be. He's so convinced he's going to find treasure tomorrow, and he starts to tell me about all the things he's going to get. A new house, a car, an air conditioner. I let him talk me out of leaving, and then

I hate myself the next day. So this time I'm just going to go."

Outside, a plane roared overhead, sounding as if it was barely higher than the rooftops. Even though I couldn't see it, I knew it was the weekly mosquito plane, spraying the bogs and swamps with insecticide. Mom pulled some tissues out of her pocket and blew her nose. She patted the bed next to her and I sat down. Then she hugged me and started to cry. It was weird how we both knew that I was staying. In a way I felt a little hurt that she didn't at least ask if I wanted to go, but I guess there was no sense in pretending. She squeezed me hard and the dampness of her tears seeped through my shirt to my shoulder. I guess I was still kind of stunned by the whole thing.

"You've seen how he's changed," Mom said. "He's like a gambler going back every day for that one big score. He doesn't care what he looks like, or where he lives, or how his family suffers. I don't think he even realizes how addicted he is."

"Like Grandma and Grandpa," I said.

"Just like them. Maybe I should've known. Even back in Flintville. The lottery tickets. And the poker games. But it just didn't seem that bad." She kept hugging me and running her fingers through my hair. "Please don't think I'm being selfish."

"I don't, Mom. You stayed here a long time."

"You'll come up and see me, won't you?"

"Sure."

"Promise?"

"I swear."

We heard Betty's car outside. Mom wiped her eyes and got up. That's when it hit me that she was really going. I couldn't quite believe it. But then she got the suitcase and we went outside. I thought maybe she'd stop and take one last look at the Shack, but she went out the gate and got into the car without glancing back. She stuck her arms out the window and sort of hugged my head.

"I love you, hon," she whispered, choking on her tears. "Please don't forget that."

"I—I won't, Mom."

"I'll call."

"You better."

She hugged me again. Her eyes were wet and red. "Bye, hon."

"Wait, Mom," I said. For one second she gave me this incredibly hopeful look. Like she thought I'd decided to go with her.

"I just want you to know," I said. "It's not like I'm choosing between you and Dad. It's Flintville or Key West. Know what I mean?"

Mom nodded and dabbed her eyes with a tissue. The next thing I knew the car was rolling down Ashe Street. I still couldn't believe she was really leaving, but then the car was gone. After a while I sat down on the curb and looked at the sky. The clouds were wispy and shaped like long white feathers. Cutting through them was the silver speck of an Air Force jet leaving a thin white vapor trail. I thought about this book called *Just Me and My Dad* my parents used to read to me when I was a kid. It was a story about a father taking his kid camping. They pitch a tent and catch a fish and sit around the campfire telling ghost stories. Sometimes I used to pretend that it really was that way, that Dad and I lived by ourselves and Mom wasn't around. It was fun to pretend because when I was finished I could always go back to having a mother and a father. As I watched the clouds I knew I wouldn't have to pretend anymore.

I was still sitting on the curb when Dad got back from diving. I could tell he hadn't found anything that day. It had been so long that even an old spoon would have been cause for excitement. In the basket of his bike was an underwater metal detector. There must have been something wrong with it that he hoped he could fix.

It's funny how someone can gradually change and if you see them every day you don't really notice it. Mom's departure made me remember the first trip we'd taken to Key West and how Dad had looked like a normal, clean-shaven Spanish teacher. Now he looked like a vagrant, with his uncombed hair and wild beard and his old clothes covered with grease marks and holes.

"Hey, whatcha doing out here?" He got off the

bike and went into the Shack. Mom was usually at work by now so he didn't notice that anything was wrong. I went in and sat down at the kitchen table. Dad was opening a can of Campbell's Chunky Chicken Soup.

"Hungry?" he asked.

"Mom left," I said.

Dad stopped turning the can opener. He looked a little stunned. I guess he could tell by the tone of my voice that I didn't mean she'd left for work. "When?" he asked.

"This afternoon."

"What'd she say?"

"Grandma had a heart attack. But she said she's not coming back."

He sat down across from me and clasped his hands together. They were full of cuts and scrapes. The nails and cuticles were black from dirt and grease.

"Why couldn't she wait?" he asked. "This always happens. We go through a dry spell, then we have some finds, then we go through a dry spell again. It always gets better."

"I guess she felt she'd waited long enough," I said.

"And haven't we had finds?" Dad asked. "Haven't we found treasure?"

"It's not that, Dad," I said. "She never liked it here. We all knew." For the first time in my life I didn't feel so much like his kid as his equal.

Dad stared at a spot on the table and said nothing.

After a while I finished making the soup and got out some bread and cheese.

"I know I could've been better," Dad said, sipping a spoonful of soup. "But it's not like I forced her to move down here. She wanted to write."

"I know."

"Every time I thought about taking some time off, or putting some money into the house, I . . . felt like I was just prolonging the search. Ultimately making it harder on everyone. Maybe I was kidding myself, but I honestly believed the best way to make her happy was to find the treasure as fast as possible."

He was giving me his side just as Mom had given me hers. I could've blamed him for making Mom so miserable, just as I could've blamed her for leaving. But mostly I just wanted them to get back together. Dad and I sat at the table, staring into our soup bowls. As it turned out, neither of us had much of an appetite.

"You don't think you'll get divorced, do you?" I asked later as I put the dishes in the sink.

The question seemed to startle Dad. "Did she say that?"

"No, but . . . isn't that what happens?"

"God, I hope not. I mean, maybe she just needs some time by herself. Don't be so fatalistic, Chris. She could be back in a week or two."

I squirted some dish-washing liquid into the sink and ran the hot water. "I don't know, Dad."

"That's right. We don't know. People change their minds. The important thing is to let her know we want her back. Whenever she's ready, the door's open."

"How about us going back to Flintville?" I asked.

He shook his head. "No."

"Why not, Dad?"

"I'm not sure I can explain it, Chris," he said, taking a deep breath and letting it out slowly. "Ever since we came down here that time on vacation, I knew this was where I had to be. As if everything else I'd ever done was just preparation. I look back at my life . . . why I taught Spanish and coached swimming. It seemed like I had the pieces of a puzzle but couldn't put them together. Now I know how the puzzle fits. The ship came from Spain and I have to dive to find it. The treasure is the last piece. Does that make sense?"

"Like you were born to do it?"

"In a strange way, yes."

It sounded a little weird to me, but I didn't argue. Dad obviously believed it, and who was I to say it wasn't so? I started to rinse the dishes. Dad sat at the kitchen table and worked on the metal detector. He'd opened a beer. I'd noticed lately that he'd been drinking a lot.

Around three in the morning I woke up and heard him on the phone with Mom. He must've stayed up and waited until she got to her parents' house in Flintville. He asked how long she thought she'd be gone. I don't know what she answered, but Dad was quiet for a long time. After a while he said, "Well, I just want you to know that I love you. You take as much time as you want. Just stay in touch."

12

Two months passed and Mom didn't return. On the phone she said she'd gotten her old job at the newspaper back. Christmas vacation came and along with it a round-trip plane ticket to New York. I was freezing by the time I got to Flintville. It was in the low forties, and I could remember days when I'd gone out in only a sweater in that kind of weather. But after living in Key West it felt frigid. On the way home from the airport Mom stopped at a mall and bought me a down jacket.

I can't say I was thrilled about going to Mom's parents' house. It was a big old place in the nicest part of town, but it was boring. Mom's ancestors settled in Flintville before the Civil War, and her great-grandfather had been mayor during the 1920s and 1930s. Her father used to teach history at the community college, and her mother had been president of the Flintville Historical Society. Dad said Mom's family had once had some money, but over the years most of it had been spent. All they had left were these dusty old scrapbooks and diaries that were supposed to prove how important Mom's family had been to the history of Flintville.

Since the heart attack Mom's mother had been confined to a special bed with an oxygen tank beside it. Grandpa sat in a chair in the corner with a book in his lap. Half the time he was asleep. Christmas morning we exchanged gifts around Grandma's bed. I got a mountain bike and a computer-game system.

It seemed like Mom had something special planned every day. One day it was a trip to New York City to see the Museum of Natural History and the

Christmas tree at Rockefeller Center. Another day we went ice fishing with the sports editor from the newspaper. Then we went away skiing for two days in Vermont. I got the feeling that Mom was trying hard to show me how great living in Flintville could be.

On New Year's Eve she took me to a party over in Philipsburg at a big house with an indoor pool. While the adults were upstairs all the kids had a pool party. I have to admit it was fun.

The next morning we didn't get up until eleven. I was scheduled to fly back to Miami late that afternoon. Mom made French toast, Canadian bacon, and fresh orange juice, which just happens to be my favorite breakfast. We sat in the breakfast nook surrounded on three sides by the bay window. It was snowing, and in the backyard two deer were nosing around in the grass.

"I bet you haven't had a breakfast like this since we moved," Mom said.

"Maybe the fresh orange juice a few times," I said.

She smiled. "I've talked to Mr. Piattoni, and he said it would be fine if you wanted to come back to school for the spring semester."

"You mean stay here in Flintville?"

Mom nodded. The look in her eyes was halfway between hope and tears. Ever since Christmas morning I'd had a feeling this was what she was driving at.

It wasn't like I was supposed to pack up that bike and computer system and take them back with me.

"How about you coming back to Key West?" I asked.

She shook her head. The smile was gone.

"How come?"

"I'm not a waitress, hon. I'm a newspaper editor. Maybe I could've lived in that miserable little house if I'd had a good job. But I had nothing. No job, no home, no friends. I was lonely and bored and all we did was fight. It wasn't good for you. It wasn't good for us. I didn't see any reason for it to improve."

"Think you'll ever come back?" I asked.

"Why can't he come back here?"

I told her Dad's story about the puzzle and feeling that he belonged in Key West. Mom rolled her eyes but didn't say anything.

"I thought if two people loved each other it didn't matter where they lived," I said.

Pressing her coffee mug between her hands, Mom gave me a sympathetic look. "I used to think that too."

We finished breakfast without saying anything more about it. I realized that in the back of my mind I expected that someday Mom would come back to Key West so we could be a family again. After our talk I got the feeling she wouldn't. I tried to hide the fact that it made me feel pretty bad. I mean, how important could a job be? More important than me?

* * *

Back in Key West nothing had changed. The *Treasure Hunter* was still at Lester's Boat Yard. The *Dolphin* was still anchored out at the treasure site, blasting empty craters in the sea bottom whenever Dad could scrape together enough cash for a drum of diesel fuel. More than a year had passed since the last piece of treasure had been found.

Instead of being depressed, Dad was full of hope. He had a new plan and was running ads in the Miami *Herald* for "Investors Interested in the Treasure of a Lifetime." He was going to rent the banquet room in a Holiday Inn up in Miami, get a bunch of investors together, and sell them shares of stock in a new company called Treasure Hunters, Inc.

On the morning of the big day, Shannon, Betty, Tom, Dad, and I assembled in front of the Shack. Dad had gotten a haircut and was wearing his brown suit. He'd borrowed some of the best pieces of treasure back from coin dealers and put them in rented display cases, which were covered with blankets and lying in the back of Tom's pickup. Dad would ride with Tom. Shannon and I got in Betty's car.

We followed Tom out to A1A and headed north toward Miami, squinting in the bright morning sun. The license plate on Tom's pickup, held on by wire, flapped in the breeze.

"You realize there must be thousands of dollars'

worth of treasure in the back of that old pickup?"
Betty said. "I hope your dad knows what he's doing."

"That makes two of us," I said.

At the Holiday Inn in Miami two security guards
helped us carry the display cases into the banquet
room. Then they stood guard while we rushed
around getting the room ready. Dad set up a slide
projector and screen. Betty, Shannon, and I put out
cookies and punch. Tom got up on the stage behind
the lectern and checked the sound system while four
maintenance men put out three hundred chairs.

"I hope someone comes," I mumbled as I pulled
the plastic wrapping off the platters of cookies.

"Look at it this way," Shannon said, licking confec-
tioners' sugar off her fingers. "If they don't, you'll get
to eat all these cookies."

"Yeah, but they may be all I eat for a long time," I
said.

The meeting was scheduled for 4 P.M. At 3:30 an
old guy wearing a light blue shirt and matching pants
wandered in and picked up a cookie from the snack
table. Tom started to tell him the room wasn't open
yet, but before he could finish Dad rushed over.

"Now, Tom, I think we can make an exception for
this gentleman," he said.

The man smiled as he chewed on the cookie.

"Your name, sir?" Dad asked.

"Fernland," the man said. "Joe Fernland."

"Well, Mr. Fernland," Dad said, "I'm glad you could make it here today. Have you seen the treasure yet?"

"Nope."

"I think this will interest you." Dad put his hand on Mr. Fernland's shoulder and led him toward the display cases. Tom gazed at the ceiling and shook his head.

By 4 P.M. the room was packed, mostly with people my grandparents' age. Almost all of them went straight for the refreshments. By 4:15 every cookie had been eaten and the punch bowls were drained.

"You'd think they hadn't eaten in a week," Betty whispered.

Afterward, they crowded around the display cases. All the best and most interesting pieces were there: Bobby Clark's gold bar, the gold cup with the winged mermaid, gold chains, and silver and gold coins. All together it looked pretty spectacular, and once again I regretted that Dad had sold it all to raise money. Especially since the money was now gone.

When we got everyone seated Dad stood at the lectern and told them how we'd found the treasure and what the Spanish treasure galleons of the 1600s had carried.

"It was not uncommon for a galleon to carry more than eighty troy tons of gold and silver," he said with great flourish. "That amount today would probably be worth nearly a billion dollars!"

There were gasps and murmurs in the audience. Next, Dad showed slides of galleons in storms with their sails torn and rigging smashed. Then he showed diagrams of the scatter pattern.

"The pieces we've found so far should lead to the main treasure hold," Dad said, "where most of the gold and silver will be."

After the slide show Dad explained how the investment worked. "For a mere thousand dollars you can own part of a treasure that could be worth a million!"

There were more murmurs in the audience. Betty turned to me and whispered, "Sounds pretty good. If I had an extra thousand, I'd buy in."

Dad asked if there were any questions, and that's when the man sitting in the middle of the audience stood up. He had a thick brown mustache and wire-rimmed glasses and was wearing a big red button shaped like a stop sign with STOP 'EM printed in white letters.

"Mr. Cooper," he said with a southern accent, "my name's Ed Bargelt and I represent an organization called STOP 'EM, which stands for Stop Taking Old People's Hard-Earned Money. Speaking plainly, sir, the purpose of our organization is to make sure elderly people living on fixed incomes aren't hoodwinked or conned into unsound investments. Now, I don't mean to imply that your offering is unsound, Mr. Cooper, but before these folks here start writin' out thousand-dollar checks, I think there's a couple of things they should be aware of. Would you mind if I asked you some questions, sir?"

"Not at all," Dad said.

"Well, first of all, you say that for a thousand dollars these folks can buy a share of treasure potentially worth up to a million."

"That's right," Dad said.

Mr. Bargelt turned to the crowd. "Now, folks, think about this commonsense-wise. If you had something you thought might be worth up to a million dollars, would you be willin' to part with it for a mere thousand?"

People shook their heads.

"Well, let me explain," Dad said. "First of all, I said it *could* be worth up to a million dollars per share, but it may turn out to be less and there's always a chance no treasure will be found at all, although based on what we've found already, I find that an unlikely possibility. Secondly, to be frank, I'm pretty low on funds right now. I need money to keep looking for treasure, so I have to take what I can get."

"All right," Mr. Bargelt said. "Those are not unreasonable replies. But let's continue for a moment. Now you say there's a huge amount of treasure lying somewhere on the ocean floor. Now how do you know that to be a fact?"

Dad explained how he'd had the coins authenticated and how, according to history, the fleet of 1632 had been captured by the Dutch, and why this led him to believe that one of the ships had escaped, only to be driven into the reef by a hurricane.

"But this is all based on supposition," Mr. Bargelt said. "You have no proof that such a galleon actually existed. You have not seen this galleon, nor do you know anyone who has. You haven't found any record of it. In fact, you don't even have a name for it. You just *think* it's there."

The crowd began to mumble. For the first time Dad looked uncomfortable. He cleared his throat and fidgeted. "Well, that's true. But the treasure I've shown you today had to come from somewhere."

"Yes, and I've done some research into that," Mr. Bargelt said. "What I've discovered is that thousands of galleons sank along the coast of Florida, but only a handful were treasure galleons. How do you know the treasure you found wasn't just the private possessions of a few rich individuals on one of those regular old galleons?"

Dad began to explain how the clump of nearly mint silver coins he'd found must have come from a treasure galleon, but it was too little too late. The audience was murmuring and people were starting to leave. Those who stayed seemed more interested in talking to Mr. Bargelt about STOP 'EM than listening to my father.

By 5:30 the banquet room was empty and Dad hadn't sold a single share. Tom, Betty, Shannon, and I carried the empty platters and punch bowls out to the cars and then helped move the display cases. When we returned Dad was sitting on the edge of the stage, staring at the empty seats. His tie was open and his hair was messed up.

Betty gave me a nudge. "Go talk to him, Chris."

I wasn't eager to do it. I figured he must have been really mad and disappointed. I walked over and stopped a few feet away.

"Guess you're pretty ticked at that guy, huh?" I said.

Dad shook his head slowly. "He was only doing what he thought was right. I just wish I'd spoken to him *before* I planned this whole thing."

"So what are you gonna do now?" I asked.

"We've got to find out more about that ship, Chris. Where it came from, what its name was, and what it was carrying."

"How're we gonna do that?" I asked.

Dad hopped off the stage and put his arm around my shoulders. "Easy. We'll go to Spain."

13

January 24
Dear Shannon,
   I can't believe I'm in Seville. All my life I thought Spain was something that only existed in geography books. But it's real. Believe me, after a week of Spanish food I almost wish it weren't.

We've been here six days. Until two nights ago we stayed at this cheap hotel with a bathroom down the hall, which we had to share with the other guests. The first night I forgot to knock, and this old lady was inside and she screamed at me. Then two days ago we moved to a room in the Estudios Hispano-Americanos, this dingy old boardinghouse that rents rooms to students at the university. We're sharing a bathroom again, but the students don't seem to mind as much when I forget to knock.

I thought we'd do some sight-seeing, but Dad's getting right to work. Before we left Key West he got all my class assignments for the year, so I have to work too. Just my luck to have a father who's a teacher.

Every day we go to this place called the Archivo General de Indias, the General Archive of the Indies. It's in this big stone building near Plaza Triunfo, which is paved with cobblestones. You go in through these huge iron doors and up a wide marble staircase. It kind of feels like a medieval castle because the walls are covered with tapestries and portraits of kings and queens.

At the top of the stairs is this big wooden treasure chest. Must be four feet long, three feet wide, and three feet deep. Dad says there should be a hundred chests like it in the galleon we're looking for. I hope he's right.

The food here is pretty bad. All they eat for breakfast are rolls and coffee. And forget about orange juice. Dad makes tuna or sardine sandwiches for lunch. Dinner is usually chicken, French fries, and a salad. The fries are pretty good. There's no heat in our room and we don't have a TV either. I kind of hope we don't stay here too long.

So write back and tell me what's going on. Say hello to your mom and Tom and Bobby when you see them.

Best, Chris

February 1
Dear Mom,

We made it to Spain, no sweat, and we're living in a pretty decent place so you don't have to worry. Every day we go to the archives and study in the scholars' room. Dad reads old documents and I do schoolwork. You shouldn't worry about me falling behind. There's nothing to do here except study. I'll probably learn more than if I was back in Key West.

We're not the only ones in the scholars' room. There are scholars here too! We all sit around these tables lit by green lamps. Only Dad and the scholars don't read books, they read loose pieces of paper, which they pull out of fat leather folders called *legajos.*

I'm by far the youngest person there, and the first couple of days the scholars stared at me. But Dad says I shouldn't mind. It's a free country.

The *legajos* are usually about eight inches thick. Some of them are covered with dust because they haven't been touched in years. Every time Dad gets a new one we sneeze a lot. Inside each *legajo* is a pile of ragged papers. Sometimes they're filled with so many worm holes you can hardly read them. And the ink is really faded too. Each line looks like one long wavy scrawl. You can hardly tell where each word ends. I hope Dad can figure out how to read these things.

So don't worry. I'm really okay. I'm getting plenty of sleep (nothing else to do at night) and Dad and I are eating pretty good. I'm also taking my vitamins. Write back.

Love, Chris

March 16
Dear Shannon,
Thanks for the letter. I'm glad to hear the stone crab season has been good. I have to admit the Spanish food has gotten a little better. For breakfast I've been having hot chocolate and these long twisty *churros* that are basically sugar doughnuts without holes. Lunch still isn't great. We got sick of tuna and sardines so now we eat these ham-and-cheese sandwiches. Only the ham is sliced real thin and it tastes a little gamey.

I can't believe the stuff they eat here. Some shops have little birds and rabbits hanging in the windows.

Quail eggs are big, too, but the thing that really grossed me was, get this, fried baby eels. Can you believe it?

Dad's getting better at reading the *legajos,* but it's still going slow. The problem is there's tons of them, and most are totally disorganized hodgepodges. One page might be an old letter to the King of Spain reporting weather conditions in the Gulf of Mexico, the next might be a passenger list from a galleon, and the next might concern a dispute over a Mexican slave. The only thing they have in common is that they all deal with the New World.

I'm starting to wonder if he really understands what a monumental task this is going to be. I mean, this *whole building* is filled with *legajos.* We could be here forever.

Dreaming of pizza, Chris

April 21
Dear Mom,

Good news! Dad thinks he's found the ship. It's called the *Sevilla* and was part of a fleet that left Havana in late September of 1632. Four of the ships were treasure galleons carrying silver and gold from Mexico and Peru. According to historians, the whole fleet was captured by the Dutch off the coast of Florida. The thing is, Dad's discovered that some ships got away, and the *Sevilla* was one of them.

Remember that anchor we found a couple of years

ago? Dad wrote to Bobby and asked him to go out and give it a close look. He says he remembers seeing a code on the shaft of the anchor. We're hoping it might help prove that it was from the *Sevilla*.

Anyway, you really don't have to worry about my schoolwork. Dad's a teacher, remember? He's been sending my tests and book reports back to Key West. Last week I got an A— on a book report about *The Old Man and the Sea*.

And thanks for the back issues of *Sports Illustrated* and *Car and Driver*. Think you could send *Playboy* next time? I hear it has some really good articles (just kidding).

Love, Chris

May 15
Dear Bobby,

Thanks for writing back so fast with the anchor code. The good news is, Dad found the construction contract for the *Sevilla*. The bad news is, none of her anchors carried the code AE363.

Dad says the contract is still important, especially if we ever do find the remains of the *Sevilla*. It was armed with twenty cannons, more than a typical merchant ship, and that will help prove it was a treasure galleon.

I think it's great that you've decided to stay in Key West another year. Dad says not to worry about those leaks in the *Dolphin*. As long as you don't mind going out every now and then to pump her bilges, he's pretty sure she'll stay afloat until we get back.

So take care and say hello to everyone for us.

Best, Chris

14

June 20
Dear Shannon,

Great news! Dad found the *Sevilla*'s manifest and passenger list. When it left Havana in the fall of 1632, it was carrying 291 passengers, 54 troy tons of silver coins, three troy tons of gold coins and bars, and nearly 80 pounds of emeralds. We still don't know what happened to her. Dad says it's conceivable she returned to Havana. Or that she sank but was salvaged. It turns out that whenever a galleon sank, the Spanish used native divers from Mexico and the Caribbean to recover the cargo. Some of the divers could dive a hundred feet and stay down for three minutes or longer. Big lungs, huh? Dad thinks the Spanish definitely would've tried to salvage the *Sevilla,* and there should be records saying so. He's worried that those silver coins he found might have been something the salvagers missed.

Last week Dad gave me all my finals. When I finished we talked about what I would do for the summer. He wanted to make up his own assignments for me. Can you believe it? I reminded him that even in Spain students get the summers off. So instead he's going to let me help read *legajos.*

He also got this scholar named Julio to help us. He's probably in his early twenties, and you can't believe his clothes. Totally tattered. What he does for a living, if you can call it that, is research for students at the university. Like, he gets paid for doing their homework! Anyway, the university gets pretty quiet in the summer so Dad hired him to help us. Dad can only afford to pay him $5 a day, but Julio seems glad to do it.

I can't believe how fast Julio goes through these

legajos. I think Dad was worried at first that he was faking. But a couple of days ago he found the contract for the *Flora,* one of the ships that escaped from the Dutch along with the *Sevilla.* One of the *Flora*'s anchors carried the code AE363, which is the code on the anchor you and I found the day we got caught in that squall.

This is really good news because Dad thinks that if the *Flora* sank near Key West, the *Sevilla* can't be far away. The question is, where is it?

So say hello to everyone for us and fill me in on what you're doing.

> Best, Chris

August 3
Dear Mom,

I really think you're getting worked up over nothing. First of all, even though I wasn't in school last spring, I still managed to get a B average. Second, missing gym isn't the worst thing that ever happened. Third, by helping Dad read *legajos* I'm actually improving my Spanish, so if anything, it's like I'm in summer school. Fourth, Dad says he wrote to the school and they're going to send him all the books I need for next year. Fifth, I'm eating fine, drinking milk, and taking vitamins.

Dad says he doesn't want to leave until he knows precisely what happened to the *Sevilla,* but I really don't think that means he's going to stay here forever.

Want to come visit us? Now that it's stopped raining, it's pretty nice. There are flowers everywhere, on balconies, in window flowerpots, in gardens and parks. And they've got this stuff called jasmine that even blossoms at night and makes the air smell sweet. I know that's the kind of thing you like.

And it's not true that we never leave the archives. We've gone to a bullfight and a soccer match, and took a bus out into the country and visited some ancient Roman ruins. It was amazing, Mom. You study the Roman Empire in a history book, and the next thing you know you're standing in this place with these old crumbly stones and columns and all of a sudden you think, "Hey, here it is!"

So I promise I won't stop eating and I won't fall behind in my studies. And thanks for the birthday present. The pajamas are very nice, and who knows, maybe someday I'll even wear them. Keep the magazines coming. I don't know why, but I've had a real craving for Malted Milk Balls lately.

Love, Chris

September 7
Dear Shannon,

I can't believe school's started again. The other day this big cardboard box came. I was really excited until I saw the return address: Key West High School,

Key West, Florida, U.S.A. Inside was a year's supply of schoolbooks. Yuck.

The only good thing is, Dad says that each day after I finish my school assignments I can help with the search. I figure if I work really hard each morning, I can finish my assignments by lunch and have the afternoon to read *legajos*.

We haven't had any new discoveries lately. Dad and Julio are reading through the *legajos* containing salvage records for the early 1630s.

So fill me in on what's happening at school and what your new teachers are like. One of these days I'll be back.

Best, Chris

October 12
Dear Mom,

I'm still doing all my schoolwork and still eating. By the way, thanks for the Malted Milk Balls.

I can't believe it's October and I don't even know who's in the World Series. I think the first thing I'll do when I come back is get a pizza and watch about a hundred hours of TV.

Here's the latest. Dad and Julio are pretty sure the *Sevilla* sank near Key West in a huge storm. There are no salvage records, so there's a good chance she's still down there somewhere.

Halloween's coming up. Think you could save some candy corn for me?

Best, Chris

15

o Los Papeles
de
Juan Ferrer

Between the late 1400s and the mid-1700s so many galleons sank off the coast of Florida that someone once estimated there was a sunken galleon along every quarter mile of beach. The records of these ships could have filled a large swimming pool. Their pages laid end to end might have stretched to the moon.

The next two months were the most difficult ever. Desperate for new leads, Dad compared the *Sevilla*'s passenger list to her casualty list and found nine names missing. We had to assume these were the survivors. Doing the same to the *Flora*'s lists, he came up with three names. He and Julio divided up the survivors of the *Sevilla* and I got those from the *Flora.* Day after day we slogged through the *legajos* looking for those names.

At night I sometimes dreamed of galleons being tossed in a violent storm. I pictured the survivors thrown into the pitching waves, grabbing on to the torn rigging of a broken mast and later being washed up on some sandy Florida beach. During the day in the scholars' room my eyes felt strained, and sometimes, instead of reading *legajos,* I took little naps at the table. I was starting to miss Key West. Even Flintville was better than this.

Finally Dad asked me if I wanted to go home. It was night and we were lying in our beds in our little room in the Estudios Hispano-Americanos. Outside, a pouring rain beat against the tiled roofs of the surrounding buildings.

"With you?" I asked.

"I have to stay," he said.

"Why?"

"You know why. The answer to the *Sevilla* is somewhere in the archives."

"It could take years," I said.

"I know."

"So why, Dad?"

He was quiet for a moment, and we listened to the rain splattering in the window boxes and flowerpots. Then he said, "It's a question I ask myself a lot, Chris. Why did I give up teaching? Why did I drag you away from Flintville? How did I get so consumed with this search that your mom left? I know people back home must think I've gone batty. All I can tell you is that just because someone grows up and becomes a husband and a father doesn't mean he automatically knows what he wants to do with his life. He may pretend, just so his wife and son feel secure. But deep down he knows something isn't right. That's how I felt until this treasure hunt came along. I know it's been crazy, it's been painful, it's been incredibly frustrating. But the craziest thing of all, Chris, is that it's always felt right."

"What about Mom?" I asked.

In the dark I heard him sigh. "I miss her a lot."

"Then let's go back together," I said.

"I can't, Chris."

I turned over and looked out the window. The rain was running down the glass. It was November and Seville had become a gray, rainy city.

"So what do you think?" Dad asked.

"I don't know, Dad. Let me think about it some more."

* * *

I decided that if we didn't find anything by Christmas, I would go back to Flintville and start the spring semester there. Dad accepted my decision, although I could see it was painful for him. It was almost exactly a year ago that Mom had left, and now, if we didn't have some kind of miracle, I was going to leave too. Living alone in Seville wouldn't be much fun for him.

We had Thanksgiving dinner in a restaurant. Since no one in Europe celebrates that holiday, we had to settle for roast chicken. Julio and Dad had glazed looks from too many hours staring at *legajos*. We all went around squinting, and lately I'd begun to see black spots when I looked down at the pages.

In the restaurant Dad leaned on his elbow and picked at his dinner. He looked tired. "Sometimes I feel like the answer is right there in front of us. We're looking at it, but we just don't see it."

"Wouldn't it be great if there was a *legajo* called 'Sunken Treasure'?" I asked.

Dad and Julio grinned at each other. It was an amusing idea, and the first thing Dad did the next morning was submit a slip of paper on which he'd written "Sunken Treasure." The humorless *portero*, whose job it was to bring us the *legajos*, simply shook his head.

Dad shrugged. "It was worth a try." He and Julio began searching through more salvage *legajos*.

For me, reading the *legajos* had become just as

tedious as doing homework. But I felt guilty if I didn't help. At a loss for anything better to do, I requested *legajos* in the names of the *Flora*'s three survivors. I doubted any existed, but the time would pass while the *porteros* looked through the stacks. The first two requests yielded no new *legajos*. Finally, I put in a slip for Juan Ferrer, who had been a seventeen-year-old apprentice seaman when the *Flora* sank. It was late afternoon and I began to daydream about dinner. Maybe I'd have fried fish, French fries, and string beans. Or maybe flat green beans with lots of oil and garlic.

Thump! The sound of a *legajo* hitting the table startled me. But there in front of me lay *Los Papeles de Juan Ferrer,* with two hundred years' worth of dust still on it.

We were not the first treasure hunters to use the archive. Whole books about treasure had been written based on research done there. None of the salvage *legajos* ever had much dust on them because every five or ten years a different treasure hunter had gone through them looking for the story of one wreck or another. But the dust on *Los Papeles de Juan Ferrer* was so thick, I knew at once it had never been read. After all, who cared about the seventeen-year-old survivor of a merchant ship?

I did.

The Juan Ferrer I began reading about was much older than the one who survived the sinking of the

Flora. This one was thirty-nine, but the year of the documents was 1654, which would have made him seventeen in 1632. In 1654, Juan Ferrer was made the vice admiral of an armada that patrolled the coasts of Portugal and Spain, protecting Spanish galleons from the Dutch and English pirates. The Dutch were especially annoying. The Spanish called them "the beggars of the sea." Most of the documents were Ferrer's reports to the King of Spain on the fleet's activities—escorting Spanish ships, chasing away Dutch pirates, and sometimes even engaging in battles. There were no rules on the open seas. It was strictly finders-keepers and survival of the fittest. For hundreds of years the Spanish had ruled the Atlantic, but by the time Ferrer became vice admiral, Spain was like a former heavyweight boxing champion demanding respect but not getting any. Twice Ferrer's own ships sank in the middle of engagements, but he must have been pretty successful because in the next set of papers he was no longer a vice admiral but a full-fledged admiral.

It took me a long time to get through this *legajo.* Instead of skimming it, looking for key words like *Sevilla, Flora, la tormenta* (storm), and *la plata* (silver), I was actually trying to read it. Days passed. I'm not sure I really believed I'd find any information about the treasure. Instead, I was just curious about Juan Ferrer's life.

The week before Christmas Dad went to a travel

agency and bought my ticket home. By then I was sure I wanted to go. I felt bad leaving him alone in Spain, and I was worried that he might never come back, but I knew I couldn't change his mind. Hopeless as the search sometimes seemed, it was what he wanted to do. I was also reaching the end of Juan Ferrer's *legajo*. Ferrer had served the King of Spain faithfully and was rewarded finally with the governorship of a part of Mexico called the Yucatán. Toward the end I found a series of letters describing his preparation for his journey back to the New World:

I wish to arrive in Mérida by the fifth of September. However, it is impossible to predict the weather at that time of year. Forty-two years ago I was extremely fortunate to survive attack by the Dutch and a heinous series of storms that destroyed the ship I was apprenticed on, the *Flora*, as well as the treasure galleon *Sevilla*. I still remember watching the *Sevilla* disappear from sight perhaps half a league to the east from where the *Flora* had run aground on a sandbar. I think the *Sevilla* must have broken apart completely, for two days later, after my rescue by Cuban fishermen, we sailed over the very place she went down and it was as if she'd never been there. The *Flora* herself was washed off the sandbar and sank, taking nearly 200 lives with her.

I looked across the table at Dad and Julio, hunched over *legajos,* squinting, tracing the faded lines of script with their fingers.

"Hey," I whispered, sliding Ferrer's letter toward them, "Merry Christmas."

16

I don't think I ever had a greater Christmas. We had no time to exchange gifts, but we were going home. It was hard to say good-bye to Julio, but Dad promised him a share of the treasure and gave him an extra $200. He rode out to the airport with us, and there were tears in his eyes as he waved good-bye.

At the airport Dad went to one pay phone to call Betty and I went to another to call Mom. It had been so long since we'd called anyone that we'd completely forgotten about the time changes and woke them in the middle of the night.

The sun was just setting when we arrived in Key West on Christmas Day. Christmas lights were strung through the coconut palms, and at one house a pelican sat on top of a plastic Santa's head. Dad and I had been traveling for close to eighteen hours, and we were bushed. As we turned the corner of Ashe Street, we saw a light on in the Shack. Dad paid the cabdriver and we dragged our stuff up the path. Through the window I saw Betty in the kitchen. She must have been making a homecoming for us. Then Shannon pushed the door open. Her hair was long and she looked older. There was something different about her, but I couldn't put my finger on it.

"Welcome back," she said. "How are you?"

"Good," I said, still trying to figure out why she looked different.

"Mom said you think you found the wreck," she said.

"On paper, at least."

"Great," she said. "I can't wait to start diving again." I could see the excitement in her eyes.

"Welcome home, boys!" Betty shouted from the kitchen. "Tom and Bobby will be by in a bit. They just went down to the store for some refreshments."

I dropped my bag in the living room and looked around. It felt weird to be back. The tiny rooms and the dank smell of damp furniture that never quite dried out. I walked back toward my room and noticed the door to Dad's bedroom was open. I peeked in and did a double-take. Mom was standing in front of the mirror, putting on makeup. Her hair was shorter than I remembered, and she was wearing a red dress.

She hugged me. "Merry Christmas, Chris."

"What're you doing here?" I gasped.

"Thought I'd come down for the celebration," she said.

Dad heard the commotion and came in. As soon as he saw Mom he stopped. Mom looked a little nervous.

"Did I do the right thing?" she asked.

"The right thing?" Dad scowled, then grinned. "Oh, yes. Hell, yes!"

I could see what was coming and started sidling out. By the time I got to the door, they were in each other's arms, making soap-opera faces. Forget the mistletoe, I thought, closing the door quietly behind me.

The celebration lasted past midnight. We had so many stories to tell about Seville and the archive, and so much to catch up on in Key West. Dad showed everyone copies of the documents we'd found—the letter from Juan Ferrer about watching the *Sevilla* sink and the ship's manifest stating the treasure she carried. With these documents he was certain he could find investors. In fact, the first person he was going to call was Ed Bargelt, the man from STOP 'EM.

Bobby looked tan and healthy. His hair was longer, and he'd added a small gold hoop earring to his right ear. He told us the *Dolphin* was still anchored over the scatter pattern and the *Treasure Hunter* was still in dry dock at Lester's waiting for an overhaul. The previous fall Tom had taken an eighteen-pound mutton snapper on the flats, the largest on record with a fly rod. Now that he had a world record his guide business had almost doubled. He looked a little heavier than before, and his khaki guiding clothes were clean and well pressed. Nothing much had changed with Betty and Shannon, except I knew what was different about her now. She was wearing makeup.

Around midnight she and I sat outside on the porch. It was a little chilly and Shannon huddled in a sweater and denim jacket. Maybe because of all those long cold days in the archive, it didn't bother me as much. All I wore was a T-shirt with a sweatshirt over it.

An unfamiliar scent hung in the air. At first I wondered if it was some Key West flower I'd forgotten about. Then I realized it was perfume.

"How're the crawfish this year?" I asked.

"I don't know. I didn't put out my traps."

That surprised me. "How're you gonna save for your trawler?"

Shannon gave me a look, and I began to realize that a lot had changed while I was away.

"So, who have you been hanging around with?" I asked.

"Oh, no one," she said.

"No one?"

"Well, sometimes I do things with David."

"David Lester?" I don't know why, but I was sort of dismayed to hear that. "What kind of things?"

"Oh, I don't know. We've gone to the movies a couple of times. And he's teaching me to drive. That's all."

"You sure?" I asked.

Shannon rolled her eyes. "Yes, Chris, I'm sure."

Knowing Dad, I expected him to start looking for the *Sevilla* the very next morning. But he and Mom slept late and then went to the Pier House for brunch. They asked if I wanted to come, but they were being so lovey-dovey and touchy-feely that it would have been an embarrassment to sit at the same table with them.

Instead, Shannon, Bobby, a girl he knew named Tammi, and I took Shannon's skiff out to the *Dolphin* for a picnic.

"Bet you missed diving," Bobby yelled over the

drone of the outboard as we raced down the channel past Crawfish Key.

"You know it," I shouted back, glad to be out on the water again, bouncing over the waves and feeling the wind in my face.

"Maybe you better put on some sun block," Tammi told me. She was short and pixieish, with curly black hair and a big smile. I looked down at my arms and was surprised at how pasty my skin was. After eleven months in the scholars' room, I'd become a real pale-face.

Still, I waved the idea away. "Naw, I gotta get tan again sooner or later."

Just past Rock Key the *Dolphin* came into view. She was listing badly. I quickly looked back at Bobby.

"Don't worry," he shouted. "She's always like that when I come out here. I'll get the bilge pump going and she'll be level in ten minutes."

"Still can't find the leak?" I asked.

"Must be just at the water level," Bobby said. "I swear I've been over that hull five times."

As we got closer something else began to bother me. I couldn't believe what a mess the *Dolphin* was. Rusted from top to bottom, holes all over the place, all kinds of junk lashed to her sides.

"What's the matter?" Shannon asked, reading my expression.

"Did the *Dolphin* always look this bad?" I asked.

"I don't remember it looking any better," she said.

I shook my head in wonder. Somehow during the time I'd been away I'd managed to have her painted and fixed up in my mind.

We pulled alongside and Bobby hopped up on the deck, which must have been on a twenty-degree angle. We watched him scamper over to the pump and give the cord a few pulls.

The engine started and soon the *Dolphin* began to right itself, and the rest of us climbed aboard. I walked to the stern and looked out over the water, blue as far as the eye could see. Bobby slapped me on the back.

"How's it feel?"

"Good." I grinned. "Great."

The water temperature was around sixty-eight, which meant full wet suits for everyone. I tried to pull on my old suit, but I had a problem. "Hey, this doesn't fit anymore."

"Must've shrunk," Bobby said. Tammi giggled. I went to find a bigger suit.

A few minutes later I splashed in and felt the water envelop me. Feeling weightless for the first time in almost a year was great. This was my home, even more than the Shack.

We teamed up—Shannon and I, Bobby and Tammi —and swam toward the reef. Each of us had a spear gun and a mesh bag to hold lobsters and any fish we caught. As we approached the reef I felt my excitement grow. Darting in and out of the green coral and purple sea fans were hundreds of tiny, brightly colored fish, the same ones I used to see in aquariums up north. Whole schools of lemon fish and yellowtails swam by. There were parrot fish in every iridescent color—turquoise, yellow, bright green, lavender, hot pink, and royal blue—nipping at the coral with their funny-looking beak mouths. Sea turtles swam lazily by and fearsome barracuda hung motionless, watching us. I saw my first crawfish scurry under a coral head and followed it. Suddenly a big green moray eel shot out, its mouth open and needle-sharp teeth bared like a cat hissing. I backed away fast.

A moment later I saw a second lobster under a rock and managed to flush him out with the tip of my spear. After stuffing him into the bag attached to my waist, I turned around in time to see Shannon chase another lobster across the sandy bottom. It was a good thing these Florida lobsters didn't have big claws like their cousins up north or we'd never have been able to grab them.

The crawfish were plentiful inside the reef, and it wasn't long before we each had three. Shannon pointed at her spear gun, indicating that it was time to find a grouper.

We swam together, spears ready. A brilliant blue parrot fish ignored us, knowing instinctively that we wouldn't spear it. Angel fish and purple spottails darted in and out of the coral. Out of the corner of my right eye I saw a big grouper slip under a coral shelf. From the sluggish way it swam, I could tell it was vaguely aware that trouble was brewing but not yet convinced that serious evasive action was necessary. Shannon went down under the shelf. A cloud of sand kicked up and a moment later she backed out, pulling the line from the spear gun. At the end of the line was the grouper, impaled in the side, jerking back and forth.

We were headed back toward the *Dolphin* when I sensed that something was wrong. The water around us was suddenly deserted. Shannon sensed it too. We both stopped swimming. All of a sudden a nine-foot hammerhead shark appeared fifty feet away, its tail swishing slowly back and forth as it glided through the water. We watched motionless, hoping the shark wouldn't notice us. But the grouper was still kicking in Shannon's mesh bag, and a small stream of blood was escaping from the spear hole. That hammerhead wasn't leaving until it ate.

Shannon opened the bag and let the wounded grouper escape. No sooner was the crippled fish freed than the hammerhead wheeled around and charged. The grouper couldn't have been more than ten feet from us when the shark's jaws snapped down around it. In a flash the shark was gone. Shannon and I made bug eyes at each other. Talk about close calls.

We started swimming quickly back to the *Dolphin*, eager to get out of the water. About forty feet from the ship I sensed we weren't alone. The hammerhead was back, making a wide circle around us. Normally the shark should have been happy with the grouper, but circling like that wasn't normal. Circling is what sharks do before they attack.

Keeping a wary eye on him, we continued toward the *Dolphin.* Hammerheads are definitely man-eaters, though not as dangerous as the great white and tiger sharks, which often attack without provocation. We tried to swim without any sudden or awkward movements. The more we resembled big healthy fish, the less likely the hammerhead would charge.

As we neared the ship the shark made another pass, this time only twenty feet away. Every muscle in my body tensed. My mind kept telling me that the shark shouldn't attack. It had just eaten, and neither Shannon nor I were bleeding. Yet somehow I knew I was wrong. Aware that the shark's tough hide was practically impenetrable, I held up my spear gun anyway. It was the only protection we had.

The hammerhead made its final turn just as we reached the side of the *Dolphin* and Shannon began to climb up. I kept telling myself it wouldn't attack. There was no logical reason. . . . The next thing I knew it came straight at us, mouth opened, white teeth bared. I shut my eyes and shoved the spear gun forward, praying I'd get him in the snout.

BANG! My head felt like giant cymbals had smashed around it. Ears throbbing, I opened my eyes and saw what appeared to be a stunned hammerhead shark jerking spasmodically in the cloudy water. Then a hand grabbed my air tank and pulled me backward. Still groggy, I half climbed and was half pulled onto the *Dolphin*'s deck.

"You okay?" Bobby's face was only a few inches from mine, but he sounded as if he were a hundred yards away. Bells were ringing in my ears. Shannon and Tammi, still in their wet suits, were giving me concerned looks. On the deck near them was the bang stick, a ten-foot pole with a cartridge on the end. Bobby must've killed the shark with it. Being in the water when that cartridge went off was like standing next to the barrel of a shotgun. The ringing was slowly subsiding and my head was gradually starting to clear.

"I didn't have any choice," Bobby said apologetically. "It was either him or you. I figured you'd rather lose an eardrum than a leg."

People say that blood in the water attracts sharks, but loud noises attract them even faster. Even as Bobby spoke dorsal fins cut across the surface toward us. We stood at the rail of the *Dolphin* and watched the water become turbulent as crazed sharks thrashed below, taking huge bloody bites out of the hammerhead. It took no more than three minutes and then the water was calm again. All that remained was a thin red foam clinging to the surface.

"You sure you're okay?" Bobby asked, patting me on the shoulder.

"Except for the bells," I replied, gazing at the reddish cloud in the water.

Later we beached on the lee side of Coral Key and built a fire out of driftwood. Tammi had speared a big grouper, and we stuffed it with lobster, mushrooms, shallots, and tarragon and cooked it in lemon juice.

We sat around the fire, eating the fish with our fingers and talking about the future now that Dad had proof the *Sevilla* existed.

"In a couple of months we could all be rich," Bobby said dreamily.

"What do you think you'll do if we find it?" Shannon asked him.

"Oh, I don't know," Bobby said, picking his teeth with a fish bone. "Set up my parents so they'll be comfortable. Maybe hire someone to help take care of them. Then I'd try to talk Chris's dad into hunting for more treasure. There's a galleon that caught fire and burned off the coast of Costa Rica. They say it carried twice the treasure of the *Sevilla,* but it's in eight hundred feet of water. Maybe we could get one of those minisubs with the mechanical arms."

"But if the *Sevilla*'s treasure made you rich, why bother?" Tammi asked.

" 'Cause it's not the money," Bobby said. "It's the adventure, the gamble. I grew up with a mother who couldn't see and a father who couldn't walk. You know what the biggest problem in our house was? Finding stuff. Especially with four kids running around. Somebody was always missing a tennis shoe, or the baby's pacifier wasn't where it should've been. I just loved looking for stuff. That was my role in the family. I was the finder."

"So you're just doing what you did as a kid," Tammi said.

"Darn straight," Bobby said with a grin. "Except now we've all grown up and left home, so I get to look for bigger and better stuff."

A pelican was standing fifteen feet away, like a dog waiting for table scraps. Bobby tossed it the grouper's tail. The bird caught it in the air, tilted its head back, and swallowed. The tail lodged in the pelican's skinny neck, making a big fishtail-shaped bulge in its throat just like a cartoon character.

"What would *you* do if we found the treasure?" Bobby asked Shannon.

"Go to college," she said. "And then just travel everywhere. Europe, Africa, Asia. There's a huge world out there and we've seen so little of it. I'd get one of those unlimited airline tickets that lets you go to as many places as you like, and when I was finished I'd go back to the place I'd liked the best and live there."

They turned and looked at me.

"No way," I said, shaking my head. The others gave me funny looks. "Seriously. It's bad luck to talk about it. Like counting your chickens before they hatch."

Bobby laughed. "Listen to this guy. Mr. Superstition. I mean, come on, Chris, we know it's here. We could probably load some gear into the skiff and take a look this afternoon."

"We wouldn't find anything without the prop ducts," I said.

"You never know," Bobby said with a glint in his eye. He looked at the girls. "Whatdya say?"

Tammi and Shannon were game so I went along, not wanting to spoil anyone's fun. There was a lot of ocean bottom half a league from the *Flora*'s anchor, and I couldn't imagine what they hoped to find. But we went back out to the *Dolphin,* got our gear, and ran east in the skiff for about a mile and a half until Bobby found a spot that "smelled good."

We put on our tanks and dived. The water was about fifty feet deep, and just as I'd feared, the bottom was flat, sandy, and empty. Bobby tried to sweep the sand aside with his hands, but there might have been ten or fifteen feet of it and brushing away a few inches wasn't going to make a difference. Gradually we all headed up to the surface and climbed back into the skiff.

"Well, at least we got to see where we'll be diving," Bobby said optimistically as he pulled off his mask. He started the skiff's engine, but we didn't move.

"What's the problem?" Tammi asked from the bow.

"Don't know," Bobby said, scowling. "She was running fine before, and now all of sudden I can't get her into gear."

He tried again but couldn't get the engine into forward or reverse. Finally we took off the engine cover and looked inside.

"Anyone know anything about the gear shifts in these things?" Bobby asked.

Shannon and I shook our heads.

"Then I guess it's time to start rowing." He threw the oars into the oarlocks and pointed the skiff east. It was around three in the afternoon and we were about twelve miles from Key West. We settled into our seats and watched Bobby pull on the oars. Meanwhile, Shannon had a funny smile on her face. Sort of like the *Mona Lisa*.

"What is it?" I asked.

"Welcome back to Key West," she said.

17

Taking turns with the oars, we must've rowed a couple of hours before we flagged down a sponge boat and got a tow home. By then I'd been out in the sun all day and my skin was bright red. As soon as Betty saw me she went out behind her house and cut a bunch of aloe leaves. Then she and Mom spread the sap right onto my sunburn. Even with that and a lot of aspirin, that first night was hell. One minute I'd feel chilled to the bone, the next minute I'd be burning up. I don't think I slept more than an hour the whole night.

They kept me in bed the next day. By then my skin had started to blister and I looked like a second-rate movie alien. To keep me in aloe sap, Betty defoliated just about every aloe plant in her backyard. As I lay in bed something else disturbed me almost as much as the sunburn. I hadn't been back in Key West seventy-two hours and already I'd been attacked by a shark, had engine trouble, and gotten a bad sunburn. It was dumb to be superstitious, but still . . .

On the morning Mom was supposed to return to Flintville, I went into the bedroom where she was packing.

"Feeling better?" she asked as she folded her clothes into her suitcase.

"Lots." The burning sensation was gone and my skin had just started to peel.

"You better use that sun block until you build up a tan," she said.

"How come you're going back?" I asked.

Mom looked surprised. "I don't have a choice, Chris. They expect me at work Monday morning."

"But you and Dad have been getting along pretty good."

I could see she had no easy answer. Maybe I was wrong to pry, but it was weird that she was living in Flintville and Dad was living here and yet they loved each other. Maybe it would've been easier for me if they'd acted like they really hated each other. At least then I could understand them wanting to be apart.

A small, crooked smile appeared on Mom's face. "I know this doesn't seem fair to you," she said, fingering the latch on the suitcase. "For the first fifteen years of your life you had a stable home and two parents who were always there to love and take care of you. I'm sorry I can't stay, hon. Really I am. All I can tell you is, I love you and I love him, but I just can't live here."

"So what's going to happen?" I asked, peeling a sheet of skin the size of a baseball card off my shoulder.

"Ick! Don't do that." Mom shuddered.

"You're just gonna see each other on vacations?" I asked.

Mom's eyes started to get watery. "Hon, please don't make it harder than it already is."

Now that we had proof the *Sevilla* had gone down near Key West, Dad was able to find new investors. Soon it was like old times again. Teams of divers, under Bobby's direction, began working from the *Dolphin.* On weekends Shannon and I joined them.

Within weeks we began to make new discoveries. Bobby found a line of ballast stones like the kind ship builders laid in the galleon bottoms to make them stable in rough seas. A galleon with a huge gash in its bottom would spill ballast stones like beans falling out of a broken beanbag. A new diver named Ellen found a heavy gold chain, which had probably been worn by one of the *Sevilla*'s rich passengers. Shannon found a large copper pot that might have been used in the galley. But nothing we found pinpointed the precise location of the *Sevilla* or her treasure hold.

By the middle of March the *Treasure Hunter*'s engines had been overhauled and she was ready to return to work. Dad, Shannon, and I left Key West at daybreak to sail her out to the treasure site. She smelled of turpentine and machine oil, and her engines purred.

By the time we got to the site the *Dolphin*'s ducts were already digging craters and the first team of divers was in the water. The second team was sitting on the rusty deck in the shade of a makeshift tarp, eating cereal and drinking coffee. Bobby was filling tanks at the compressor.

"Any luck?" Dad called as we came alongside. Bobby shook his head. Dad turned to the charts in the *Treasure Hunter*'s cabin and studied them.

"What'd you have for dinner last night?" Shannon asked Bobby.

"Grouper, what else?" he said.

"Any sharks around?" I asked.

Bobby shook his head. His jaw was covered with blond stubble, as if he was growing a beard.

"When was the last time you were onshore?" Shannon asked him.

"Oh, uh . . ." Bobby thought for a moment. "About three weeks ago."

"Don't you want to go back?"

Bobby shook his head and grinned. "You kidding? I want to find that darn treasure."

Dad came out of the *Treasure Hunter*'s cabin. "I'm going to go up near the reef and try the line from Billow's Shoal to Black Key."

"Good luck, Captain." Bobby saluted him.

Dad turned the *Treasure Hunter* around and headed to the new spot. It had been nearly two weeks since we'd found anything, and I could feel that gnawing, worried sensation. Were we on the brink of another long dry spell? Would Dad run out of money again? We'd been searching for more than four years. How many more would it take?

We ran toward Billow's Shoal. Off the starboard beam the ocean waves were breaking over the outer reef. I could almost read Dad's mind. Once the *Sevilla* hit the reef, how far did it drift? Where did it finally sink? Dad picked a spot and anchored. The depth finder said we were in about thirty-five feet of water. Dad put the prop ducts down and started blasting. Shannon and I dived over the side.

On the bottom the water around the crater was full of churning sand. Shannon caught my arm and pointed up. Above us a big cloud of sand floated close to the surface, catching the sunlight and sparkling like Tinkerbell's fairy dust.

By now the prop wash had reached bedrock and the crater was widening. I could see that it was empty. Soon the rim of the crater stopped growing. Well, I thought, it was only the first of many craters we'd look into that day. No reason to get discouraged. Yet.

I was halfway back to the surface when I realized that Shannon wasn't with me. Automatically assuming the worst, I hurried back down and saw her floating about two feet off the bottom at the very edge of the crater. She was almost motionless, and fear seized me for a moment. But then a long stream of bubbles poured out of her regulator and I knew she was breathing.

I swam closer, and a moment later I, too, was hanging motionless in the water. Directly under Shannon the bedrock changed colors—from gray to bronze. It was unreal. I knew what color that bronze would be at the surface. Gold. Pure gold.

The gold began at the edge of the crater. We started brushing the sand away with our hands and there was more—a rug of gold lying on the sea bottom. I tapped Shannon on the head and gave her the thumbs-up sign. Even with the regulator in her mouth, I could see that she was grinning. I grabbed one of the coins and swam up.

Had it been only a few feet to the surface, I probably would have shouted with joy when I got there, but having thirty feet to go gave me time to plot my announcement. My heart was pounding like mad and I felt short of breath, but when I got to the surface I tried to look bored. Dad leaned against the stern.

"What do you say we drift down about fifty feet and try again?" he asked.

"I wouldn't go that far," I said, treading water and clenching the gold coin in my fist. "Try about fifteen feet."

Dad scowled. "How come?"

"No real reason," I said. "It's just that the whole bottom over there is covered with gold."

He just stared at me. I guess he was so used to no news that the good news didn't make sense.

"Don't joke with me, Chris."

That's when I held up the gold coin. It glinted in the sunlight, and Dad's mouth fell open. The next thing I knew he dashed into the cabin and grabbed a mask and flippers. A moment later he vaulted over the stern and free-dived with just the air in his lungs to sustain him. I followed him down. By the time we got to the bottom, Shannon had swept away more sand, revealing hundreds and hundreds of gold coins. Dad reached down, took two handfuls, and let them fall, tinkling against the others. He reached for my mouthpiece and took a couple of breaths, as if he couldn't bear to leave. Shannon was still sweeping the sand away and uncovering more coins. By now there must have been six square feet of them covering the bottom. Dad even picked one up and bit into it, just to be sure it was real.

We finally swam up to the surface and radioed Bobby to bring the *Dolphin*. Diving back to the bottom, we tied mesh bags to ropes and started filling them with coins. Soon the divers from the *Dolphin* joined us and for the next two hours we filled those bags again and again.

By midafternoon the crater was empty. On the *Dolphin*, Bobby blasted more craters but didn't find any more treasure. We left him and his crew at the site and headed back to Key West in the Mako.

We had about 850 gold coins, each one weighing nearly an ounce. In sheer weight alone that was probably about $400,000 in gold, but as rare coins they were worth much more. Dad got on the radio to Tom and used a code they'd made up years ago.

"Tom, we finally got that tuna," Dad said.

"Tuna?" Tom's voice was staticky over the radio. *"Oh! The tuna! Well doggone! Is she big?"*

"Figure eight hundred at least," Dad said.

Tom whistled over the radio.

"I was thinking about a little reception down at the dock," Dad said. "What do you say?"

"I'll get right on it," Tom said. *"And congratulations, Ted. It's been a long time coming."*

It was late afternoon when we got in. Waiting at the dock for us were the police chief, two of his officers, the president of the First Keys Bank, Tom, Betty, and about two dozen curious onlookers. As soon as we'd docked, Tom and Betty shook up bottles of champagne and popped the corks, showering us as if we'd just won the Super Bowl. We put the coins in the trunk of the police car and went over to the bank. Everyone waited outside while Dad, the bank president, and the police carried the coins inside in a wheelbarrow. About ten minutes later they came back out. Dad had a huge smile on his face.

The celebration that night was a lot smaller and quieter than I'd expected, just Tom, Betty, Shannon, and us. Bobby and the other divers were still out on the *Dolphin*, eagerly waiting for the sun to rise so they could look for more treasure. And even though the gold was safe in the bank, I think Dad was a little nervous about spreading the news. In the Shack, he opened another bottle of champagne and we all had a little, even Betty.

"Here's to finding the *Sevilla*," Tom said, raising a mug filled with champagne. But before we could toast, he lowered it. "Oops, can I say that?"

"Well, we've got a chestful of gold coins all dated

1632," Dad said. "I can't imagine that it came off any other ship."

"But is finding a chest of gold the same as finding the ship?" Betty asked.

Dad thought it over and raised his glass. "Let's just toast the gold."

The party ended early and everyone went home, eager to get a good night's sleep before diving the next day. I went into the bathroom and washed up. When I came out Dad was standing at the kitchen sink, his wrists covered with suds as he washed the dishes, his shoulder propping the phone against his ear.

"Nope, I couldn't even begin to guess," he was saying. "But you know that shearling coat you've always wanted? Why don't you go out and get it. . . . Better yet, why don't you get it and then hop on a plane down here and help me celebrate for a week? What? . . . No, there's no rush. . . . Okay, let me know. . . . Yup, Chris sends his love. He's doing great. I'll tell him. I love you, hon, and I miss you. Get that plane ticket, okay? Bye."

He hung up.

"Mom?" I asked.

"Yup. She sends her love." Dad had the biggest smile on his face.

"You think this is it, huh?"

"Well, you saw the ship's manifest," he said, drying

his hands with the dishtowel. "There have to be a couple of dozen more chests just like that one."

"Think you'll find more tomorrow?" I asked.

"I think we have a good shot," he said, putting his arm around my shoulders. "Any gambler'll tell you, Chris, luck tends to run in streaks."

I got up early the next morning and dressed in cutoffs and a T-shirt. Dad was already in the kitchen, pouring water into the coffee machine.

"What are you doing?" he asked when he saw me.

"Going diving," I said.

"Today's Monday, smart guy. You're going to school."

"You can't be serious," I argued. "We're on a lucky streak. What if we find the rest of the treasure this week? Are you really going to make me miss this historic occasion on account of school?"

Dad smiled. "Get into your school clothes."

"But what do I need to go to school for?" I asked. "We're rich."

Dad stopped smiling. "First of all, we're not rich. A large part of that gold has to be sold to pay off loans and investors. What's left will have to pay for diving until we find the rest of the treasure. And if we ever do get rich, it's going to mean that you'll be able to go to college. In the meantime you don't know what we're going to find this week and neither do I, and I'm not about to let you miss school looking for it."

"Mom'd let me dive."

"Don't give me that," Dad said sharply. "If any-thing, your mother's stricter than I am. And I don't like you playing us off against each other."

I was in my room changing into my school clothes when someone knocked on the front door. Chair legs scraped the floor as Dad got up. Then the door creaked.

"Mr. Cooper?" a voice said. "Jack Lapwood from the Associated Press. I was wondering if I could have a word with you."

I stuck my head out into the hall. Jack Lapwood was wearing a jacket and tie and was holding a micro-phone up to Dad's face. Before Dad could answer, a van screeched to a stop out in the street. "Hey! Wait a second!" a guy in a blue suit cried as he hopped out.

I ducked back into my room and pulled on the rest of my clothes. When I came out Jack Lapwood was pressing the microphone closer to Dad's face. "Can you tell me what you found yesterday?"

"Well, uh, we found some gold," Dad began to say. Outside, another car pulled up. Meanwhile, a TV crew from the van was trying to get through the gate, but some of their wires got caught.

"Don't start the interview!" the guy in the blue suit shouted. He looked like a TV news reporter.

The woman from the third car didn't even bother with the gate. She just hopped the fence and tried to fight her way through the palms and vines to the porch.

"When you say some gold," Lapwood was saying, "can you be clearer? Can you give an amount?"

"What'd he say?" called the woman climbing through the vines.

"If you'd shut up for a second, maybe you'd hear," Lapwood snapped at her.

I don't think Dad knew what to do. He just stood there, stunned that news of the discovery had spread so quickly. Meanwhile, the TV crew got to the porch, and the guy in the blue suit was trying to muscle his way past Lapwood. Dad seemed frozen and I knew I had to do something. I'd seen it done on TV plenty of times.

"Listen, guys," I said, sliding into the doorway. "Give us a couple of minutes and we'll have a statement." Then I slammed the door.

Inside, Dad looked confused. "I don't want to give a statement."

"Then don't," I said. "There's no rule."

Someone banged on the door. "Mr. Cooper? I really need to speak to you now. I've got a deadline."

"But it's their job," Dad said, looking back at the door.

"Don't worry, Dad. I have a feeling they'll get the story whether you give it to them or not."

The newsmen kept banging on the door. Dad and I snuck out the back and cut through yards until we came out on White Street. We were jogging down the sidewalk toward the marina when Dad stopped.

"Wait a minute." He pointed toward Key West High School. "You're going that way."

"But you need someone to deal with the media," I said.

"Don't worry," he said with a smirk, "I'll handle it."

18

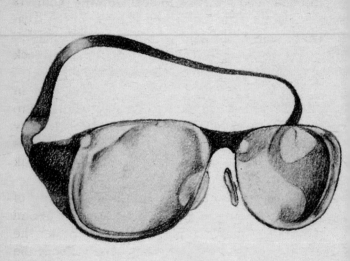

SUNKEN TREASURE FOUND

KEY WEST, Feb. 11 (AP) —A "rug of gold coins" found on the sea bottom this week may be the beginning of a major new treasure find near this resort town, according to a former New York

Spanish teacher who is hunting for the ship the gold came from.

"We've found some gold. Now we've got to find the ship," said Ted Cooper, the former Spanish teacher who heads Treasure Hunters Inc., a company he formed to hunt for the treasure.

Experts estimate the total take from the wreck could run into "the hundreds of millions."

Mr. Cooper said he spent almost a year in Spain researching the sunken ship before coming here to dive. While he refused to give any details about the ship, local experts say the coins probably came from a Spanish galleon that sank in the early 1600s.

"Those galleons carried enormous amounts of treasure," said Dr. Alfred Sonfer of the Miami Oceanographic Institute. "If Cooper locates the main treasure hold of the ship, the value of the find could be staggering. . . ."

Almost overnight things went crazy. As soon as the news stories appeared, would-be treasure hunters started showing up at our doorstep, begging for a chance to dive. Strangers came by claiming to be coin dealers and asking to see the doubloons. The phone never stopped. People called from Texas, California, even Alaska. Crackpot inventors claimed they had devices that could locate gold half a mile away. A few people begged for money, and still others just wanted to talk to someone "famous." If we took the phone off the hook, they knocked on the door. Dad put a "Beware of Guard Dog" sign on the gate, but it didn't fool anyone. Finally we checked into a motel and went into hiding.

Out at the treasure site dozens of boats came around every day. According to the admiralty injunction no one except Dad's divers were supposed to take treasure from the area, but that didn't mean people couldn't swim down and look. Bobby complained that the ocean floor was swarming with other divers "just watching."

Dad was so busy he had to rent a little office in town over the Blue Parrot bar. All day long, instead of diving, he'd be on the phone, or holding business meetings, or trying to deal with all the weirdos who demanded his time. Even some of his legitimate investors came down and had to be taken out to the treasure site, given tours of Key West, and wined and dined in fancy restaurants like the Pier House and Coral Lodge.

One afternoon after school I came back to the motel and found him talking on the phone to Mom.

"I wish you'd come down," he was saying. "I've got so much going on I can't keep track of it all. I can't even dive I'm so busy here. I need someone to organize things. . . . What? No, but . . . I know I could hire a secretary, but that's not the point. I want you.

. . . But you could get a great story out of it. A book even. 'The Discovery of the *Sevilla*.' . . . You mean you just want to work on that newspaper forever? . . . Okay, bring your mother with you. . . . Keys Memorial is a fine hospital. . . . Well, I'm sorry you feel that way."

He hung up and lay back on the bed. He had dark rings under his eyes. His cheeks were sunken and I could have sworn his hair was turning grayer.

"She won't come?" I asked.

"Nope." Dad slid his hands under his head and stared up at the soundproof tiles in the ceiling. I guess there wasn't much to say that we hadn't already said. I gazed out the window at the pool in the courtyard. Some tourists were lying on the lounges, relaxing, getting tan. I really didn't know what was keeping my parents apart. Stubbornness? Pride? Or maybe they really needed to be doing exactly what they were doing, and it was just too bad there wasn't a shipwreck up near Flintville or a newspaper job for Mom in Key West. I heard a snort and turned to look at Dad. He'd fallen asleep. In the middle of the afternoon.

I had to get used to people staring and sometimes even pointing at me. At school the stares came from kids in other grades, since by then most of the kids in my grade knew what my father did. Ever since I'd come back from Spain I'd been getting a lot of double takes, too, as if I looked familiar but kids couldn't quite place me.

Things had changed at school. Most of the girls wore makeup, and the guys all talked about cars now. Some, like Billy Peebles and David Lester, had even bought their own cars with the money they'd made from shrimping. They'd drive their friends to school in the mornings, and on the weekends they'd run up US1 to Marathon and Islamorada, although just what they did up there was anyone's guess.

One morning I was getting on my bike to go to school when Shannon came out of her house. She'd made her hair wavy and was wearing makeup. Something else was different, and it took me a moment to realize she was wearing a skirt.

"Come on," I said. "Get your bike."

"Uh, I've got some things to do," she said. "You better go ahead."

"There's time," I said. "I'll wait."

Before she could reply, David drove around the corner in a Suzuki jeep and stopped in front of her. Shannon glanced sheepishly at me. David pushed open the passenger door for her and nodded at me. He was wearing blue-tinted sunglasses.

"Well, uh, I'll see you at school, Chris," Shannon said, almost apologetically, as she climbed into the jeep.

I wasn't sure how I felt. Shannon was my friend, but I didn't own her or anything. She was free to do what she pleased. At the same time, the jeep did have two empty seats in back.

Shannon pulled the door closed and I expected David to drive away, but instead he let the jeep roll up to me and then stopped.

"Any finds lately?" he asked, resting his arms on the steering wheel and tipping up his sunglasses.

I shook my head. Several weeks had passed since Shannon had uncovered the rug of gold, but not a single new coin had been found. Everyone was puzzled. We knew the *Sevilla* had carried many chests of gold and silver. It didn't seem possible that a single chest could have fallen to the ocean floor without others being somewhere nearby.

"So what happens now?" David asked.

"We just keep looking."

David smiled. "What a life."

"It's okay," I said, playing it low-key.

Down the street a bunch of little kids raced by on bikes on their way to school. David looked at my bike and frowned. "Want a ride?"

I glanced at Shannon and then back at him. "You sure?"

"Why wouldn't I be?" he asked.

A few moments later I was riding in the back of the jeep, holding on to the roll bar. In front of me Shannon had pulled on a baseball cap to keep her hair from blowing around. I'd always thought of her as a good friend and diving companion. But seeing her

that morning with her hair waved and wearing a
skirt made me realize there was more to Shannon
than that. Apparently David had noticed this too.

The student parking lot at Key West High was a big
scene every morning. Driving or getting a ride to
school was considered major status, and the kids kept
an eye on who arrived with whom. Even some kids
who biked or took the bus came by just to watch.
That morning I guess it was noted that I arrived with
David and Shannon. A few spaces down from us Billy
Peebles pulled up in his beat-up Camaro, heavy
metal music pounding out of the speakers. During
the year I'd been in Spain he'd grown several inches,
lost some weight, and gained a tattoo of an alligator
on his right bicep. He and his friends still wore their
denim vests, only now their breast pockets bulged
with packs of Marlboros. Billy glanced at us and his
eyes stayed on me for a moment, as if registering the
fact that David had given me a ride. I waited for him
to utter some unimaginative insult, but he just
turned and sauntered toward school with his bud-
dies.

"Your biggest fan," Shannon whispered, nudging
me with her elbow.

19

Some kids' lives revolved around school or sports, but mine still centered on the search. As the weeks passed and no new treasure was found, it almost seemed as if the *Sevilla* had left that one chest of gold on the sea bottom and then vanished. By now Dad's divers had covered a large part of the scatter pattern. With a new high-speed magnetometer and side-scanning sonar, all kinds of relics from the *Sevilla* should have been discovered: anchors, cannons, more piles of ballast stones. Instead, they'd found nothing. As the excitement of the rug of gold began to wear off, so did the phone calls and the crazies. Dad was disappointed, but I think he was also relieved that life was getting back to normal. We even moved back into the Shack.

Trying new tacks, Dad hired a meteorologist to chart the direction of the storm that wrecked the *Sevilla* and *Flora* in 1632. He wrote to Julio in Spain and asked him to resume searching the *legajos* for clues. He even ran ads in the local paper asking if any fishermen or divers recalled coming across anchors or cannons in the area we were searching.

Another month passed with no finds. Dad began talking about another trip north to find more investors.

"But we've got all those gold coins," I said.

"The coin dealers are having a hard time selling them," he explained. "I've hit a problem I never expected. As far as collectors are concerned, the value of a coin is based on its rarity. Those eight hundred doubloons could be worth five thousand dollars apiece right now, but I might find another ten thousand coins, and then each one isn't going to be worth as much. I've heard that a lot of collectors are waiting until I either find the rest of the treasure or give up."

Two weeks later Dad got a haircut, put on his suit, and left. I went to school as usual and ate dinner with Shannon and Betty. On Friday night David invited us over. His house was one of the few in the old town of Key West that had a grass lawn instead of being over-run with vines. From the outside it looked big and old-fashioned, with French doors, gables, and a gin-gerbread railing going all the way around the second floor. But inside it had central air-conditioning and a kitchen filled with modern appliances.

We ate chips and drank pop, watched a rerun of *Miami Vice,* and played eight ball on his regulation-size pool table. At first I wondered if David had in-vited me over because he thought Shannon wouldn't go to his house alone, but he didn't ignore me or try to monopolize her. Instead he acted normal and friendly. I'd been living in Key West for almost five years, and with the exception of Shannon, he was the first kid to invite me into his home.

David's parents had gone out for the evening, and they returned just as Shannon and I were getting ready to leave. When David said he wanted to intro-duce us I felt a little nervous, but Mr. Lester shook my hand and seemed honestly pleased.

"Oh, yes," he said, giving me an appraising eye. "David's talked about you. And I know your father's boat. The one with those funny contraptions on the stern."

"The prop ducts," I said.

"So how's the search coming?" Mr. Lester asked.

"Pretty well," I said, not wanting to go into the details.

"Good," Mr. Lester said. "I hope he keeps it up. We could use a little excitement around here."

Later, as Shannon and I walked home, I mentioned that I was surprised the Lesters had been so nice.

"Why shouldn't they be?" she asked.

"Well, you know, Dad used to have trouble with the charter captains down at the marina. And I had those hassles at school. I guess we assumed people here didn't like us."

"Maybe they had to get to know you first."

"Even Billy Peebles?"

Shannon shrugged. "I don't think Billy likes anyone."

I dropped her at her house and walked over to mine. I wasn't particularly nervous about being alone while Dad was away. Betty was next door, and the houses were so close together, nothing really bad could happen without her hearing. I went into Dad's room and turned on the light. His window was open. That was weird, but I closed it so the mosquitoes wouldn't get in and then didn't think about it. Instead I sat down on the bed and dialed Mom's number. Several weeks had passed since I'd last spoken to her.

A woman answered. I didn't recognize her voice.

"Uh, hi, is Ann Cooper there?" I asked.

"No, she went out with Mr. Gifford," the woman said. "But I expect her back soon."

Mr. Gifford? I thought. Who's that?

"Is there a message?" the woman asked.

"Yes. Would you tell her Chris called?"

"Certainly."

I hung up the phone and started to get up. As I did I glanced at the mirror on the closet door. Suddenly I froze. There were two people in the mirror—me and someone tall with a mustache. I started to turn around. A second later everything went black.

I woke up in a hospital bed, my head throbbing and my throat parched. It must have been early morning because everything was quiet and orange sunlight was coming through the window. The bed next to mine was empty, but Shannon was sleeping in a chair with a denim jacket covering her. Someone down the hall was snoring.

The first thing I did was wiggle my toes. Then I moved my legs. I brought my hands up and looked at them. An IV needle was taped into the back of my left hand, but other than that I was still in one piece. By then I knew there was a bandage around my head. My left eye felt swollen, and when I touched the throbbing area above my eyebrow, it exploded with pain. Yeow!

My mouth was dry and had an awful chemical taste. A paper cup was sitting on the night table next to the bed and I reached for it, hoping it might contain some water. Unfortunately my aim wasn't too good. The cup tipped over and fell to the floor.

Across the room Shannon stirred and opened her eyes.

"You should've slept in the bed," I said, pointing to the one next to me.

Shannon blinked. "You're awake?"

"I guess I could be talking in my sleep," I said.

She rubbed her eyes and looked around. "Where's my mom?"

"You got me," I said. "What happened?"

"You won't believe it," she said, getting up. "Let me find Mom."

"Listen, before you go, think you could get me a cup of water? I've got the worst taste in my mouth."

Shannon got me the water. As she handed it to me she leaned forward and kissed me on the cheek. Something really strange must have happened.

A moment later she returned with her mother. Betty's eyes were puffy with sleep and she yawned. "I fell asleep in the lounge. How do you feel?"

"Except for my head, not bad," I said. "I'd really like to know what happened."

Betty started to explain. Someone broke into my

house and hit me on the head. Then they ransacked the place. In the process, either on purpose or accidentally, they turned on a gas jet on the stove.

"Your mom called our house around midnight," Betty said. "She'd tried to return your call, and when no one answered she got worried. I sent Shannon over and she found you. The doctor said another fifteen minutes with that gas and you would have been a goner."

"Sheeze," I mumbled.

"I wasn't able to find your dad," Betty said. "I'll have to try again this morning."

A detective arrived later that afternoon and asked me some questions, but I wasn't much help. The burglar hit me before I got a good look at him. I asked the detective if he thought they'd catch the guy, but he didn't seem too hopeful. I hadn't been badly hurt and there'd been no treasure in the Shack. As far as the police were concerned, there were more serious crimes to investigate.

That night I was sitting in bed, finishing the hospital dinner, when Mom walked in carrying a suitcase. She must have hopped a jet to Miami and caught the last flight to Key West. When she saw me her face got sort of twisted, like she wanted to cry but was too angry.

"I'm okay, Mom," I said, hoping to calm her.

"I never should've let you stay here with him," she

muttered. "He left you alone. A sixteen-year-old boy."

"Betty and Shannon live ten feet away," I said. "They're practically in the next room."

Mom was too angry to listen. "I should've known something like this would happen. And don't tell me you're okay. I know about the gas."

"It was probably an accident," I said. "The guy must've been looking in the kitchen and bumped into the burner."

Her eyes widened. It was the same look she'd given me when I was six and told her I wanted to jump off the roof and fly like a bird. As if I hadn't grown up a day in between.

"Does anyone know where your father is?" she asked.

"Betty said she was going to try to find him," I said.

"Why didn't she try last night?"

"Jeez, Mom, take it easy," I said. "She was probably too busy with me."

"Oh, that's just great!" Mom shouted. "He goes off, leaves a child alone, and doesn't even tell anyone where he's gone."

"I'm not a child," I said angrily. "And stop yelling. It makes my head hurt."

Mom sat down on the bed and took my hand in hers. "Do you . . . have any idea how I'd feel if something happened to you? You are the single most precious thing in my life, and I let you live like a . . .

hippie or something down here with an irresponsible man who can't think about anything except his stupid treasure."

"You don't have to get so angry," I said. "I mean, maybe you should be happy I'm okay."

That seemed to calm her. She looked down at my hand as if she were reading my palm. Under the nails and around the cuticles my fingers were black from grease and grime that never seemed to come off.

"I am happy, Chris," she admitted. A tear rolled out of her eye and down her cheek. "I'm extraordinarily happy that you're all right . . . but you came too close."

She stayed late and then went to a motel. I guess there was no way she was going to stay in the Shack. First thing in the morning she was back, watching over me as I ate breakfast. Around eleven the doctor came in, took the bandage off, and looked at my head. He shone a light in my eyes, then told Mom I had nothing worse than a slight concussion and was free to leave. As I got dressed I looked at myself in the mirror. I had two black eyes and a big gauze pad over the left side of my forehead.

"How long before I can dive?" I asked.

"Two weeks," he said.

Dad was coming through the lobby as we got off the elevator on the ground floor. His suit was wrinkled and his tie loosened, as if he'd been traveling all night. He was jogging, the soles of his business shoes slapping on the tile floor. About twenty feet from us he stopped.

"I'm okay, Dad," I said.

His eyes got watery as he stepped forward, glanced at Mom, and then hugged me hard. It was slightly embarrassing. He hadn't hugged me like that since I was a little kid. Finally he straightened up and pressed his fingers into the corners of his eyes. He gave Mom a quick hug, but she didn't hug him back.

"The doctor says it's a slight concussion," she said stiffly.

"What do you say we go to the Pier House for lunch?" Dad asked.

Mom hesitated and then nodded. I could tell she still had a lot on her mind. It started coming out in the cab from the hospital.

"I'm taking him back to Flintville," she stated, almost as if I weren't there. I could see that she was getting ready for a big fight.

"Don't you think that should be his decision?" Dad replied.

"No. He doesn't have the judgment. All he knows is he's having a good time here. He doesn't see the dangers."

"Dangers?" Dad asked skeptically. "Don't houses get burgled in Flintville too?"

"Yes, but criminals there won't assume he lives in a house filled with gold doubloons."

At the entrance to the Pier House they paused for

a short truce. Inside, I was surprised at how many people came over and asked if I was all right. The story of my "accident" must have spread pretty quickly. I didn't recognize many of the well-wishers, but they spoke to Dad as if they knew him. When had he become a celebrity?

We took a table overlooking the harbor. A few wispy clouds hung in the blue noon sky. Out on the water a dozen boats and sailboats cruised by. It must have seemed like a serene setting, but at the table I sensed a volcano was about to erupt again.

"I'm serious about what I said before," Mom insisted. "This has to change."

"You're right." Dad surprised us by agreeing.

Mom gave him a puzzled look.

"Everything's changed," Dad said. "It was stupid of me not to recognize it sooner." He leaned forward in his chair and gestured at some of the people who'd said hello to us. "You think they'd be so friendly if they knew I was in hock for a quarter of a million bucks?"

Mom and I stared at him. "Are you serious?"

"Dead serious," Dad said. "And that's just the loans I have to pay back. It doesn't include all the investors who expect a return too."

"What about the gold coins?" Mom asked.

"Selling just enough to pay for fuel and supplies," he explained.

"Then what are you going to do?"

"Only one thing I can do," Dad said. "Find that treasure."

Two days later we said good-bye forever to the Shack. Mom had some vacation time coming, and she hung around and helped us load our suitcases, lamps, window fans, and fishing rods into the back of Tom's pickup. It was kind of sad to leave that little house. I know it sounds hokey, but I started thinking about all the things that had happened there. Like the time Dad came home with the hunk of silver coins and the party the night Bobby found the gold bar. It was hard to believe I'd lived there almost five years.

Dad said our new living arrangement would be a surprise.

"Come on, Dad," I begged when we'd finished loading the pickup. "Tell me."

"Suppose you could live at any resort on this island, which would you pick?" Dad asked.

I looked at Mom and Tom. Tom was grinning because he already knew the answer. Mom's face was stony. She was still upset about my "accident."

"Let's see," I said. "The Pier House is pretty nice, but it's a little too touristy. The Casa Marina's got a good beach, but I guess I'd pick the Coral Lodge."

Dad smiled.

"You're kidding!" I gasped.

"Nope."

"But how?"

"I'll tell you on the way over."

The Coral Lodge had once been the most famous resort in Key West, and all sorts of rich people and movie stars had stayed there. In recent years it had gotten a little run down, but new owners had bought it and were trying to make it glamorous again.

"After we found the gold coins the owners asked me if they could put some on display in the lodge," Dad explained in the pickup. "They think the treasure could be a big attraction, especially for their restaurant business. Of course they assured me it would be in a burglarproof case with an alarm wired directly to the police station."

A few moments later we rode down the cobblestone driveway, lined with tall Alexandra palms, and stopped at the guardhouse. Dad spoke to the guard, who opened the iron gate and let us in.

We drove past the colorful gardens and perfectly trimmed hedges, past shiny new Rolls-Royces, Mercedes, and Jags. The lodge was an old four-story Spanish-style building right on the beach. It was pink stucco with a red tile roof. We passed the big swimming pool with rows of blue-and-white lounges all around it and the man-made beach with special white sand shipped in from the Caribbean. The beach was lined with coconut palms, and I'd heard that it was raked every morning to get rid of the seaweed and other stuff that drifted up during the night. An orange-and-yellow catamaran was pulled up on the sand, and fifty yards out a girl on a sailboard was skimming across the water.

"Well, what do you think?" Dad asked.

"It's great," I said. "But where are we gonna live?"

He pointed down the beach. Nestled in the palms on either side of the lodge were small pink bungalows that were usually rented to families. Mom and I looked at him like he was crazy. Two days ago he'd told us he was in debt for a quarter of a million dollars.

"It's free," Dad explained, "in return for lending them the treasure. And as you saw, it's well guarded."

I couldn't believe what I was hearing. It was like being told I was moving to paradise. "And I can use the pool and the sailboats and everything?"

"Everything," Dad said.

"And my friends can come?"

Dad nodded.

"Great!"

Mom crossed her arms, her lips pressed together in a thin line. "I guess this kills any chance of you moving back to Flintville."

"I guess so, Mom." It was hard not to grin.

20

We spent the rest of the day moving in. It was early June and the resort was pretty empty, but the few guests who were there gave us funny looks as we unloaded our stuff from the pickup. I noticed right away that the bungalow we were in wasn't as nice as the others. The outside walls were cracked and patched. The porch was uneven. There were cracks on the interior walls too.

"What's with this place?" I asked.

"It's built over an old septic tank," Dad said. "So it's slowly sinking. But there's nothing wrong with it, if you don't mind the uneven floors."

I must've looked a little disappointed, because Dad grinned and said, "Hey, come on, what do you expect for free?"

He was right. And besides, the kitchen appliances were new and the screens didn't have holes. *It even had air-conditioning!*

The June weather was warm and beautiful, and Mom stayed around for a few days, her mood gradually improving. I guess it was hard not to enjoy the beach and pool. At night, when Dad got back from his office over the Blue Parrot, she'd make dinner. Dad and I could see she liked it there.

"Why don't you stay?" I asked after dinner one night. The temperature had hit 92 that day, but we were cool and comfortable in our air-conditioned kitchen. Through the window I could see the waves lapping gently at the edge of the beach just thirty feet away.

She shook her head. "I can't. It would be too easy to become a vegetable here."

"You could work with me," Dad said.

"You need a secretary, hon," she told him. "Not me."

"But I do need you," he said.

"Aw, isn't that cute," I said.

They both gave me a look that said "Shut up." I had a feeling it was time to start studying for my geometry final the next day.

I went into my bedroom and sat down at my desk. All I wanted to do was finish my finals and start diving again. I opened my geometry book and started doing problems. The air-conditioning felt so good, I could almost taste it. Through the doorway I could see Mom and Dad sitting close to each other, talking and holding hands. By now I knew better than to get my hopes up. Nothing would keep Mom from going back to Flintville. Nothing would make Dad move from here. I'd never heard of two people being married and living so far apart, but then I'd never imagined a lot of the things that had happened since we'd moved to Key West.

A week later school ended and the doctor said I could start diving again. Dad hardly dived anymore. He spent all his time taking care of business. He had three diving boats now—the *Treasure Hunter,* the *Dolphin,* and an old dredge from the Everglades called the *Mule.* They were all decrepit.

At the treasure site Bobby stayed on the *Dolphin* for weeks at a time. He moved into the captain's cabin up on the bridge while the rest of the divers slept below in bunks. About once a week Dad would go out in the Mako and huddle with him over the oceanographic charts, trying to figure out where to dig next.

We were still going through the barren period. The treasure site looked like a battlefield filled with empty craters. Dad was always scrambling for money. Once I heard him on the phone ordering a dealer to sell his coins at any price just to get money fast. Another time I heard him speaking in Spanish and knew he was on long-distance to Julio, hoping to find a new clue to where the *Sevilla* had sunk. Week after week the same treasure sat in the display case at the Coral Lodge. The original plan had been to replace the treasure every few months to keep the guests interested. Luckily, the guests kept changing even if the treasure didn't.

June turned into July and July into August. On the days we didn't dive Shannon and I would invite David to hang around the Coral Lodge with us. But it was too hot to stay on the beach for long, and most of the time we hung out in the bungalow, playing Risk and thinking about diving again.

August ended and we had to go back to school. Dad was starting to look gaunt, as if the strain was getting to him. Sometimes he had that desperate look, like a gambler ready to sell his soul for one more bet. I began to wonder how much longer he could keep it up.

By September he had to lay off divers. In October the *Mule*'s engine blew and he had it towed back to Key West. Finally, one afternoon in November, I came home from school and found him packing a suitcase.

"Time to find more investors?" I asked.

Dad shook his head. He looked thin and his beard had started to get wild and untrimmed again. "We have to move, Chris."

"What?"

"It's coming up on high season. They can rent this bungalow for nearly two thousand a week, even with the slanted floor. My half of the deal was to put new treasure in the display case. I haven't come through, so that's it."

"But we might find new treasure any day now," I said.

Dad smiled wryly. "I've been telling them that for two months. I guess it's time to come up with a new excuse, only I can't think of a good one."

Once again we borrowed Tom's pickup and moved. Rentals got real expensive in the winter, and Dad had a hard time finding us a place to live. For a while we stayed on Tom's floor. Then finally we found a new place—an old wooden sailboat in the city marina.

"You're not serious," I groaned, standing on the

dock, staring down at the boat. The mast was gone and the blue paint on the cabin was peeling off. Under the waterline the hull was caked with barnacles and algae. A crooked, blackened stovepipe stuck out of the cabin.

"I'm afraid I am," Dad said.

"Where are we gonna wash?" I asked, knowing a sailboat that size didn't have a shower.

"The dock master's office. And you can always shower at school."

I stared at the forward deck, covered with pelican guano. "This is the pits, Dad."

He nodded. I wasn't telling him anything he didn't already know. "Listen, Chris, we're going through money faster than I ever imagined. I've got less than two hundred gold coins left. The most important thing isn't where or how we live, it's keeping the search going. We've hit hard times before. We'll get through it."

So we moved onto the sailboat. It wasn't easy. After living in the best resort in Key West, having a pool, catamarans, air-conditioning, and unlimited hot water for showers, I now had to live on a cramped, leaky sailboat and pay fifty cents for five minutes' worth of hot water in the pay shower behind the dock master's office. Maybe when I was twelve I would've considered it an adventure, but now that I was seventeen, it was just a big pain.

At Christmas, Mom came down. She took one look

at the sailboat and went straight to Betty's and slept on a couch. On New Year's Eve, Tom had a big party and a lot of the guides and charter captains came. We were really proud of him. After all those years of struggling, he was finally being accepted as a capable guide.

At midnight, all over Key West people set off fireworks. A few even fired guns. The air was pungent with the smell of gunpowder and deep-fried conch fritters. For the first time in my life I saw Dad get really drunk. He didn't get wild or loud. He just stood in the backyard, with people dancing and having fun all around him, talking about how we were going to find the rest of the *Sevilla*'s treasure any day now. The trouble was, he wasn't talking to anyone. At least not anyone Mom or I could see. We finally convinced him to lie down in Tom's bedroom. A little later, when we checked on him, he was fast asleep.

On New Year's Day the *Mule* sank at its mooring in Key West Harbor. The Coast Guard said Dad had to raise it because it was a nautical hazard. Dad said he didn't have the money. In that case, the Coast Guard said, they'd have to tow it away themselves. Dad had no choice. We never saw the *Mule* again.

In January the weather turned bad and Dad decided to call off the search for a while. The *Treasure Hunter* was put into dry dock with engine problems again, and every three days one of us would go out to the *Dolphin* and pump the bilges dry. She was al-

ways listing when we got out there. No one had ever
been able to find that leak.

By February almost a year had passed since we'd
found the rug of gold. Dad and Bobby were eager to
start diving again. The problem was, where? Julio
had recently found information indicating that the
Sevilla's captain, in a desperate attempt to keep his
ship from smashing into the reefs, might have tried
to anchor outside them. As a result Bobby had come
up with a new theory about the location of the treasure.

"We've always assumed the gold coins were from
one of the first chests to fall out of the *Sevilla* after
she hit the reef," he said one afternoon. We were
sitting around the little table in the galley of the
sailboat, the light-blue airmail letter from Julio flat-
tened out before us. Outside, it was pouring rain. The
sailboat bobbed and scraped at its mooring, and we
listened to the steady *plink plink plink* as drops
seeped through the cabin ceiling and fell into coffee
cans.

"What if that chest was actually one of the last?"
Bobby asked. "What if she sank on the outside edge
of the reef?"

"How?" Dad asked.

"Who knows?" Bobby said. "Maybe her cargo
shifted and she was already shipping water. Maybe
she took a big wave sideways and *bang!*"—he slapped

his hands together—"she hit the reef and went straight down. No scatter pattern, no nothing."

Dad sighed and shook his head.

"The point is," Bobby continued, "we've searched inside the reef with a fine-tooth comb and come up empty-handed. It's time to look someplace else."

"But the gold coins were nearly three hundred yards inside the reef," Dad said. "How do you explain that?"

"Maybe that one chest floated on a piece of debris," Bobby speculated. "Maybe some greedy Spaniard tried to sail off with it in a longboat."

Dad's eyebrows went up. "In the middle of a hurricane?"

A drop of water fell out of the ceiling and landed on Julio's letter with a *splat*. We watched it make a dark blue spot.

"Look, I don't have all the answers," Bobby admitted. "All I know is, we're running out of time and money. This isn't the time to be conservative. We have to take some risks."

Dad sat back and rubbed his face with his hands. He was tired, and I knew it had to be killing him that he'd found part of the treasure but couldn't find the rest.

"Listen," Bobby said, "you've spent six years looking for this thing. I've spent nearly four. If we had to quit and walk away right now, I'd never forgive myself for not looking outside the reef. I'd go through the rest of my life wondering, Was it there? Were we *that close*?"

"Okay," Dad sighed, "we'll dive outside the reef. But just for two weeks. I can't afford to waste more time than that."

Bobby grinned. "It won't be a waste. You'll see."

The reef line followed the Keys from the southern-most tip of Florida out into the Gulf of Mexico. The reef itself was usually ten to fifteen feet deep, although the water over some of the shoals was even shallower. To the north, what we called inside the reef, the water remained thirty to sixty feet deep for many miles. But to the south, what we called outside the reef, the ocean floor fell thousands of feet beneath the Straits of Florida.

It was difficult to anchor the *Dolphin* outside the reef. The waves were much bigger, the current stronger, and we couldn't get too close to the coral for fear of smashing on it, just as the galleons had more than three hundred years before. After half a dozen tries, Bobby finally got her securely anchored.

That weekend Shannon and I and two other divers went out in the Mako. Scott was a skinny guy with a blond ponytail who worked around Key West as a handyman. Johnny, a Jamaican, was a professional diver and part-time bartender at the Blue Parrot.

By Saturday afternoon we'd found ballast stones. Nothing indicated that they were from the *Sevilla*.

But still there was a feeling of excitement in the air. After so many barren months, at least we'd found something.

That night we cooked grouper on the deck and talked about where to dive next. Everyone was eager to explore this new area, and instead of staying up late the way we usually did on a Saturday night, we all went to sleep early. Bobby went up to his cabin and Shannon went into the supply room, where, as the only female on board, she could have some privacy. Johnny, Scott, and I settled into the bunks. I set my alarm clock for just before sunrise so that we could be in the water as soon as it turned light.

It was still dark when the alarm went off. As soon as I woke I felt the *Dolphin* listing. Johnny and Scott groaned at the sound of the alarm and kept sleeping. Waking before dawn had been a great idea, but it was a lot easier to stay in bed. Still, the ship was listing and the bilge had to be pumped out. I grabbed a flashlight.

The previous summer we'd moved the bilge pump down to the engine room. Not only was that where it belonged, but it meant you could pump out the bilge in bad weather and not get soaked. I pulled open the metal door to the engine room and turned on the light. The *Dolphin*'s two big diesels stood like a pair of greasy black oxen. The room was a mess as usual. Dirty rags, rusty wrenchs, and empty oilcans perched on every flat surface. A few inches of water sloshed around the floor, meaning the bilges had overflowed. Cans and rags floated on the surface. I slogged through the filthy water to the pump and gave the cord a pull. It wouldn't start. I tried a few more times and then checked the gas tank. It was three-quarters full. The spark plug must have been fouled.

I guess I was aware that the *Dolphin* had started to list even more, but I figured as long as I got a new spark plug in, the pump would start. Only this time, I told myself, I was definitely going to find that darn leak.

I was taking the old spark plug out when the *Dolphin* suddenly tipped farther. *Clank!* A wrench slid off a shelf, narrowly missing my head. I started working faster.

A moment later the *Dolphin* started to roll. Suddenly things were banging and smashing all over the ship. I could hear shouting above. The engine room was no place to be if the *Dolphin* capsized, so I ran for the door.

Before I could get there the whole world turned upside down. I rolled into a ball as dirty, oily water splashed over me. Something hard hit me on the shoulder. The lights went off, leaving everything black. I braced myself until the ship stopped rolling, then tried to get my footing and stood. I was knee-deep in water. Things were still banging and creaking, but the loudest sound in my ears was the echo of water sloshing around inside the hull. The *Dolphin* was upside down and I was inside her.

Pitch black. So black it made no difference whether my eyes were open or closed. I took a step. *Clunk!* My head hit something on the bottom of the *Dolphin*'s hull, now above me. I was trapped inside the boat, virtually blind, breathing the air caught under the hull. The only thing between me and freedom was an inch of steel.

For a while I think I froze with fear. I couldn't see, couldn't move without smacking into something. Maybe it wasn't real, I thought. Maybe it was the worst nightmare I'd ever had. If so, I couldn't wait for it to end.

The water snapped me out of it. It had been up to my knees before, but now it was mid-thigh and rising. The air trapped under the hull was slowly leaking out and sea water was replacing it. Pretty soon there'd be no air left.

Somewhere in the engine-room ceiling, which was now the floor, was an escape hatch. Was it on the starboard or port side? I couldn't remember. The cold March sea water reached my groin and I shivered. Was there any chance someone would come and save me? Doubtful. I didn't even know if anyone else had survived. All I knew was that if I didn't do something soon, I was going to die.

As the water rose to my waist I took a breath and dived under, trying to feel my way toward the escape hatch. But under the water and in the absolute blackness it was impossible to tell what my hands were touching. I came back to the surface. About three feet of air was left in the hull. I stood waist-deep, petrified, my eyes burning from the film of oil and gas on the water. I was trapped, I was going to die. Think, I told myself. Don't panic, *think*!

I tried to picture the escape hatch in my mind. I'd seen it a hundred times. It was square, with rounded corners, and had a red metal latch you yanked downward (upward) and turned to the right (left?). Was it closer to the bow or back toward the stern? Was it on the starboard, which was now my port, or the port, which was now my starboard?

The water was at my ribs. I dived again and again, groping blindly around the bottom for the latch. For an instant I thought I'd found it, but it wouldn't turn. Finally I ran out of breath and came up. It probably wasn't the latch at all but one of the dozens of pipes carrying water, electric lines, and engine controls from the bridge.

The water was up to my chest. How much time did I have? A few minutes? I don't know why, but I started to think about my mother and how mad she was going to be at Dad. She'd never forgive him for this. I wished there were some way I could let her know it wasn't his fault.

Then I heard a scratching sound above me, as if someone was crawling on the hull. I reached up and rapped the hull with my knuckles. Immediately someone banged back.

"It's Chris!" I shouted. "Can you hear me? I'm in the engine room."

A faint voice said something about the escape hatch.

"Can't find it!" I shouted. "Help me!"

They said something about the hatch again. I dived down, groping wildly for anything that felt like the latch, but it was impossible. The engine room must have been thirty feet long and eight feet wide. All I did was exhaust myself. I found a place to stand and gasped for breath in the remaining air. The water had reached my shoulders.

The person above was knocking again. I knocked back. Were they trying to tell me something? Or just checking to see if I was still alive?

The water slowly crept up my neck. The thought of drowning terrified me. That first and last involuntary lungful of water . . . I couldn't stand thinking about it. The knocking continued but I didn't knock back. What difference did it make? The water was up to my chin. I stretched up as far as I could and pressed my forehead against the grimy bottom of the hull. Oh, God, please, *please* don't let this happen!

The water was up to my lower lip. With my forehead pressed against the hull, I had to breathe through my nose. I began saying good-bye to everyone, apologizing to them for the unhappiness I knew this would cause. Good-bye, Mom, Dad, Shannon, Betty . . . good-bye . . .

Something floated against my chin. I grabbed it. The flashlight! How could I have forgotten it was waterproof? I flicked it on and a beam of light shot down through the murky water. I quickly pressed my lips into the remaining pocket of air and took two big breaths. Then I plunged downward, searching for the escape hatch.

I found it immediately. The red latch had been almost directly below me. I grabbed it and pulled but it didn't give. I tugged left, then right. The damn thing probably hadn't been opened in ten years. Meanwhile, I was running out of air. My lungs were starting to burn. I yanked again. It gave! I turned the latch and pushed down. The hatch opened. Suddenly there was light below me. I could see sand and some small fish swimming along the bottom. The sun had come up.

My lungs were about to burst, and I felt myself losing consciousness. I knew I didn't have the air to swim out. I scrambled back up to the air pocket.

There was only about half an inch of air left. I pressed my lips against the bottom of the hull and tried to breathe, but water ran in the corners of my mouth as I gasped for it. I got a mouthful of water and choked. *Oh no, no, no!* . . .

Something was tickling my feet. For a split second I thought it was a fish. No, they were bubbles! Bubbles of air floating up through the escape hatch and catching under the hull. I quickly pushed my face up against the hull again, gasping. First there was an inch, then two inches of it. I took breath after breath, drinking it down as if I were dying of thirst. The stream of bubbles kept pouring upward. Someone was below me, emptying a tank of air through the escape hatch.

I felt weak. Too weak to do anything except press my face upward and gasp. Air had never tasted so good. Even though the hatch was open and I was free to swim through, I could hardly move a muscle.

A hand slid around my ankle and I let myself be pulled down through the escape hatch. The water was so bright, I could hardly see, but there was a diver down there pressing a regulator between my lips. It tasted like lipstick so I knew it was Shannon.

She started to swim me up, keeping an arm around my chest and sharing the regulator. I was still weak with relief. A few moments later we broke the surface. I gulped the fresh air. God, I never knew anything could taste so good. Everything was bright, but my vision was so blurred from the gas and salt water that I could hardly see. I could hear cheering and shouts and felt hands pulling me up. The next thing I knew, I was lying on my side on the cold hull of the *Dolphin*, my head in someone's lap.

"You okay?"

"Yeah, I think so." I slowly pulled myself into a

sitting position and rubbed my eyes until I could see.
The sun was low and orange in the east. Johnny and
Scott, both bare-chested, were squatting on the hull,
shivering in the cool morning air. The water around
us was littered with debris from the *Dolphin*—tanks,
buoys, life rings, a square orange Styrofoam raft.
From the bubbles breaking the surface, I knew Shannon had gone back down. That made four of us. I
quickly looked around, but Bobby was nowhere to be
seen.

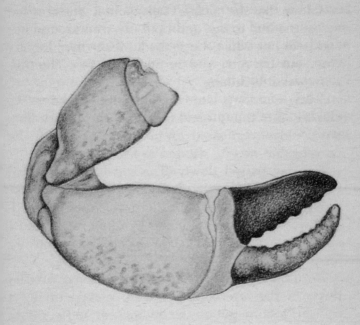

21

A few minutes later Shannon surfaced near us. I could only imagine that, because she'd been sleeping in the supply room, where the diving gear was kept, she'd been able to throw some gear on after the *Dolphin* capsized. Scott and Johnny helped her climb onto the hull.

"You find him?" Scott asked.

Shannon nodded, her face contorted with misery. I could see that she couldn't talk about it. She crawled across the hull to me, and I put my arms around her and held her while she sobbed. Meanwhile, Johnny swam out and retrieved the Styrofoam raft. The *Dolphin* was still sinking.

A few moments later the hull slipped under. We climbed into the raft and tied on to the anchor line. We could have floated toward Key West with the current, but no one wanted to leave Bobby.

The day passed slowly. The sun beat down and there was hardly any breeze. We were hungry, thirsty, and miserable, but I knew we'd be rescued. Dad was expecting me home by dinnertime, and I knew that when I didn't show up, he'd come looking for us.

We didn't even have to wait that long. Around three in the afternoon we were picked up by a trawler. Johnny put on the diving gear and got Bobby's body out of the *Dolphin*. They put him in the hold, and the trawler captain radioed the Coast Guard and Dad and told them what had happened. We huddled under blankets in the captain's cabin, sunburned and hungry but unable to eat. Johnny and Scott said they'd escaped by crawling out of portholes. Shannon acknowledged that she'd been able to throw on gear and swim out. They all wanted to know what had happened to me, but I couldn't talk about it. I just didn't want to think about how close I'd come to drowning.

"I thought for sure Bobby would get out," Scott said solemnly. "That dude was so strong."

"He almost did," said Johnny. "I found him in the hallway outside his cabin. Had about three feet to go. But with all that water rushin' in, it must've been like trying to swim up a waterfall."

After that we all got quiet again. No one involved in the search for the *Sevilla*'s treasure had ever been killed, no one had even been seriously injured. Now, all of a sudden, Bobby Clark was dead. No amount of silver and gold would ever bring him back.

Dad and Betty were waiting for us at the docks along with the police, an ambulance, and a big crowd of onlookers. They hugged us while the ambulance attendants carried a stretcher and a body bag down into the trawler's hold. We watched them bring Bobby's body out in the black rubber bag. Except for the sobbing, everyone was quiet. I'd never seen Dad look so grim and pale.

They took us back to Betty's house. We had to tell the police what happened. Shannon started to cry again. Dad sat in the kitchen, staring at the floor, his eyes watery.

"I never should've let him anchor outside the reef," he muttered later. "I should've known she'd take water too fast in those seas."

"It wasn't your fault, Dad," I said.

He just looked at me sadly, as if it didn't matter what anyone said.

Dad called Bobby's parents, and the following day Bobby's brother came from St. Louis to claim the body. He said they knew Bobby's death wasn't our fault. In his letters Bobby had always spoken of Dad with great admiration and appreciation for letting him join the treasure hunt. He'd loved being part of our "diving family."

Dad couldn't stop telling him how much we'd loved and enjoyed Bobby and how he felt sorry and responsible for what had happened. Later we took him back out to the airport. Just before he boarded his plane I asked him if he knew where Bobby's shark's tooth was.

"Is that what it is?" he asked, opening his carry-on bag and taking out the tooth, still hanging from its gold chain. He must've seen something in my eyes, because he handed it to me and said, "Why don't you take it? I'm sure it means more to you than it ever will to me."

Bobby's death cast a dark shadow over the treasure hunt. Neither Shannon nor I had ever been close to anyone who died. We talked a lot about him and what he'd meant to us. The way he was always cheerful and optimistic, ready to try almost any new adventure, but also intensely dedicated to finding the treasure.

Only in his absence did I realize that Bobby had been our mascot, our daily inspiration to keep trying. The void he left seemed impossible to fill. The *Mule* was gone, the *Treasure Hunter* was in Lester's Boat Yard awaiting another overhaul, and the *Dolphin* remained capsized on the ocean floor. No one felt like diving anyway.

A month passed. Each day I went to school and Dad went to the little office above the Blue Parrot. He talked vaguely about salvaging the electronic gear from the *Dolphin* and starting the search again, but nothing happened.

At the end of March, Dad closed down the office. Some days he didn't even bother to leave the sailboat. He'd be there in the morning when I left for school and in the afternoon when I got home. Once in a while in the evening he'd go up to the pay phone outside the dock master's office with a bunch of quarters and call Mom. One evening, after he'd finished speaking to her, he walked out to the end of the dock and leaned against a piling, looking out into the Gulf. The last orange streaks of the sunset were fading slowly away into night. I went down and joined him.

"Aren't you going to dive anymore, Dad?"

He shrugged. "I don't know, Chris. If I'd never searched for treasure, Bobby wouldn't be dead today. This search has cost more money than I ever imagined, but I never thought it would cost a life."

The running lights from a couple of boats made narrow ribbons on the surface of the Gulf. The moon was half full, and thin clouds drifted past it like gray fog past a headlight. The annual tarpon migration had begun, and out in the marina I could see an occasional set of fins slide by. Dad slid his hands into his pockets and jingled the few coins that remained from his call to Mom.

"I know the *Sevilla*'s treasure is out there somewhere," he said. "But it's a big ocean, and when you think about it, it's not much different from trying to find a needle in a haystack. We've been searching for six years, and in some ways we're not much closer than the day we started. I have to ask myself how much longer I want to keep looking, how much longer I want to keep you away from your mom, how much longer I want to live in a leaky sailboat. I could be here another six years and still not find it."

"You'd just give up, Dad?"

I don't know if he really winced or I just imagined it, but a moment later he said, "I wouldn't call it giving up. We had an adventure, did something most people never dream of doing. At this point there's enough gold left to pay off most of the loans. I'd feel bad for the investors, but they took their risks and I took mine. Everyone wants to find that pot of gold at the end of the rainbow, Chris. But sometimes you have to know when to walk away."

He put his arm around my shoulders and squeezed, then turned and walked back down the dock.

As spring came Dad spent more and more time around the sailboat. He didn't seem interested in doing much of anything, except drinking beer. If he was hungry and there was food around, he'd eat it. But if there wasn't, he'd just drink more beer. Sometimes four or five days would pass and he wouldn't shower. The sailboat smelled musty enough without his body odor, and I'd start dropping hints that maybe it was time for him to grab a towel and fifty cents and go up to the dock master's office.

It was becoming obvious that we needed money. Since Dad wasn't doing anything about it, I decided to start trapping stone crabs again. The Mako was still running, and every day after school I'd tend the traps. Most evenings it was dark by the time I came in and sold the claws to the fish market. Hauling the traps was hard work, and some nights I was so tired I went right to sleep without doing my homework. My grades at school started dropping, and a couple of teachers even asked me if things were okay at home. Everyone knew about the *Dolphin* sinking and Bobby drowning.

One afternoon Shannon came out to tend the traps

with me. She handled the Mako's controls while I grabbed the buoys and hauled the traps up. Each time I found a big beige-and-red crab inside I'd break off the larger claw and throw the crab back, leaving the smaller claw so the crab could feed and protect itself while a new claw grew. But it was getting close to the end of the stone crab season and the traps were often empty.

"I know this is none of my business, Chris," Shannon said as we moved toward the last buoy, "but what are you going to do?"

"About what?" I asked.

"About your dad and the treasure and living here," she said.

"Don't know."

"Does your mom know what's going on?"

"Sure."

Shannon cut the engine and gave me a concerned look. "Please don't lie to me, Chris."

She was right. The truth was, when Dad and I talked to Mom we both pretended things were a lot better than they really were. We never actually lied. Instead we'd just imply that we had lots of coins left and that we would be diving again soon. It's easy to fool someone when they're fifteen hundred miles away. It's a lot harder when they're sitting in a boat with you watching you pull up empty crab traps.

"I guess I'm just waiting for Dad to start diving again."

"What if he doesn't?"

I just shrugged.

We got to the last trap and I started to haul it up. The traps were made of wood and concrete, and by the end of each day my arms ached. Hand over hand, I pulled on the wet rope until the trap broke the surface. Like so many that day, it was empty. I threw in some fresh bait and let it sink.

Shannon came up to the bow and looked in the catch bucket at the day's take. "What are you getting per pound?"

"About six dollars," I said.

"I don't think you've even got a pound here."

I took a look. The claws barely covered the bottom of the bucket.

"Well," I said with a forced grin, "I guess I can always go down to Mallory Square and lie on a bed of glass."

Shannon didn't laugh. "Seriously, Chris."

I had no answer. We let the Mako drift. The sun was turning orange in the western sky, and the boat rocked gently in the afternoon breeze. At Mallory Square another batch of tourists was probably starting to gather. The guy with the bed of glass had disappeared the year before, and I had seriously considered becoming his replacement. I guess that made me realize how much a part of my life Key West had become. Now I ebbed and flowed with the tides and the seasons. Now I knew the fish, the birds, and the plant life in a way I'd never have known them in Flintville. I could understand why the conchs were so suspicious of outsiders and protective of their island.

Patches of wind rippled the glossy surface. Shannon trailed her fingers in the water. I sat down on the gunwale next to her.

"I never thanked you for saving my life," I said.

"You didn't have to."

"No, I should've," I said. "Remember that time you got your hair caught in the *Treasure Hunter*'s drive shaft? You thanked me. I feel like ever since Bobby died I've been really self-centered. Like only thinking about myself and Dad and how lousy life's been to us lately. I never ask you how you're doing. Or how your mom is. It's not right."

"I don't think it's so wrong," Shannon said. "A lot's changed in your life. Nothing's changed in mine. My mom sells jewelry and meditates. It's what she's always done and always will do. Maybe I'll go to college if we can find the money, maybe I won't. I could stay in Key West and be a trawler captain, or I could move to someplace like San Francisco and do some other kind of work. But I've got time to make up my mind. It's not something I have to decide right now. You've got things you have to deal with now, Chris. They're not going to wait."

We'd drifted near the flats behind Stock Island, and I watched a guide pole his flats skiff through the shallow water as he and his client stalked bonefish. How many places in the world could a person support himself by going fishing every day? Or by lying on a bed of glass? Or searching for treasure?

"Listen," I said, "after Mom went back to Flintville, Dad didn't have to let me stay. He could've said I had to go back with her. Everybody thinks he's totally fixated on treasure hunting, but he managed to be a pretty decent father all those years. There's no way I'm going to desert him now."

"You can't live on crab claws," Shannon said, gesturing at the bucket. "This won't even pay for the gas you used today."

"I know." I sat down at the console and started the Mako's engines. It was time to head in.

22

A few weeks later I pulled up the crab traps for the last time and quit for the season. By then I was eating half my meals at Shannon's because there was no food in the sailboat's cupboards. Betty usually made vegetarian dinners, but I must've looked pretty scrawny because one night Shannon insisted I eat there and her mother served me scrambled eggs and corned-beef hash. A few minutes later Shannon left, saying she had to run an errand in town. She was hardly out the door when Tom arrived in his pickup. I realized I'd been ambushed.

Tom and Betty stood in the living room and talked quietly for a few moments before joining me at the kitchen table.

"I never see your dad anymore," Betty said, nervously twirling a strand of hair around her finger. "How's he doing?"

"Okay," I said, between mouthfuls of hash and eggs.

They waited for me to say more, but there was nothing more to say. Tom put his elbows on the table and I caught a whiff of Old Spice after-shave. He cleared his throat. "Would you tell us what he's been doing?"

"Nothing much," I said.

They waited again. Finally Tom said, "Come on, Chris, don't be like this."

"Well, I guess he's still pretty upset about Bobby," I said. "But he's getting better. He's been talking about outfitting the *Treasure Hunter* for commercial fishing."

"Has he done anything besides talk about it?" Tom asked.

"No," I had to admit. "Not really."

Tom's forehead wrinkled and he ran his finger
pensively through his hair. You could see how wor
ried he was. I was worried, too, but there was no way
I would show that because it would only add fuel to
the fire.

"Chris, word's gotten around town that your dad
has a drinking problem," Tom said. "The reason we
wanted to talk to you isn't just because we're worried
about him. We're worried about you too."

"I'm okay," I said.

"That's not what I hear at school," Betty said.

Now I knew why Shannon had bailed out early.

"Don't be angry," Tom said. "We're just trying to
help."

"I don't need help," I said. "It's just going to take a
while until Dad decides what he wants to do. To tell
you the truth, I think he's going to start diving
again."

Tom and Betty gave me doubtful looks.

"Did you know your dad's two months behind on
his rent?" Tom asked.

I tugged on the chain around my neck and pulled
out Bobby's shark's tooth. I wore it all the time now.
If only he were still here, I thought. He could get Dad
going again.

"Chris, there are people who can help," Betty said,
leaning forward with her hands clasped. "The county
social services department could put him in a pro

gram. They might even help pay some of the bills. And they'd make sure you were taken care of."

"You mean they'd send me back to Flintville," I said.

"Not necessarily," Tom said.

I pushed my chair back and stood up. Half my dinner was still on the plate, and I would have enjoyed eating it, but Tom and Betty were making me too uncomfortable.

"Listen," I said, "I know you guys mean well, but the only thing Dad needs is to dive again. You say he's behind in his rent, but he's been in debt for a lot more than that and he's always come through."

"It's different now," Betty said, but I'd already pulled open the front door and was heading down the steps.

It was dark when I got back to the sailboat. Through a porthole I could see Dad sitting at the galley table, an open can of beer and a half-eaten bag of pretzels in front of him. I climbed on and went below. Dad nodded at me. His hair was wild and his shirt was stained. The cabin smelled of body odor and rotten garbage. On the floor next to the table was a brown shopping bag with a dozen empty beer cans in it. I sat down opposite him. It wasn't easy, because sitting at that table always reminded me of the rainy day Bobby had persuaded Dad to move the *Dolphin* outside the reef.

"We've got to end this, Dad," I said. "It's time to go back to work. We're gonna salvage the *Dolphin,* get the *Treasure Hunter* overhauled, and start diving again."

Dad looked half amused. "What're we going to do for money?"

"The same thing you've done before," I said. "Find investors."

Dad shook his head. "I've already hit everyone I know."

"Then you try people you don't know."

Dad raised an eyebrow but said nothing. He wasn't taking me seriously.

"Look, I was just over at Betty's," I said, exasperated. "She says we're two months behind in the rent. She and Tom were talking about the county social services department, like they want you to go into some kind of alcoholism program."

Dad smirked and started to lift his beer. I was suddenly so angry, I knocked it out of his hand. It bounced off the wall, and white foam and beer poured out onto the floor.

"You faker!" I shouted. "Until this year you never used to drink. Not like a drunk anyway. You're trying to make yourself an alcoholic so that everyone'll feel sorry for you. But it won't work because most of this town never wanted you here anyway. They'll just be glad when you're gone."

At first Dad looked surprised at my outburst, but then he just shrugged. "Maybe they're right."

"No!" I slapped my hand against the table, making the bag of pretzels jump. My heart was racing. I'd never raised my voice in anger at him before. But I knew I was right and I had to make him listen. "It's time to go outside the reef and see what's down there."

"Never." Dad shook his head. "There's nothing there."

"We found ballast stones."

Dad waved the words away. "No. Forget it. Worst mistake I ever made. If I'd been firm, he'd still be alive."

That was the problem. He still blamed himself for Bobby's death, and it paralyzed him. I took a deep breath and tried to calm down.

"Look, it's not your fault," I said. "Bobby dived with us because he wanted to. You didn't make him. If he hadn't dived with us, he would have dived with some other treasure hunter. Honest, Dad, what happened to Bobby is really sad, but you heard what his brother said, treasure hunting was all he ever wanted to do. And it's all you want to do too. The reason you're so lost and miserable now isn't only because Bobby died, it's because you're not diving. I don't know if you're ever going to find the treasure, Dad. All I know is you have to keep searching. Otherwise, Bobby died in vain."

Dad looked uncomfortable. He glanced around the cabin as if looking for a place to hide. Then he got up.

"Where're you going?" I asked.

"Out for a walk," he said, climbing unsteadily out of the cabin.

I followed him. Outside on the dock he looked around, as if trying to figure out where to go. It was dark and I doubted he had much money.

"Dad, you can't run away."

"Okay, enough," he snapped angrily. "I heard you."

I knew it was time to shut up, but there was one last question I had to ask. "How much rent do we owe?"

"Six hundred," he replied, and wandered away down the dock.

I was sitting in the senior lounge the next day, trying to write a paper that had been due three weeks earlier, when Shannon sat down next to me. "You're mad," she said.

"Last night I was. But not anymore."

"Why not?"

"Because you did what you thought was right. Besides, I have a lot of other things on my mind right now."

"Like what?"

"Like how I'm gonna come up with six hundred

bucks for the rent and what I'm gonna do about Dad."

"I bet my mom could lend you some money," she said.

"Thanks, but it's no good if I can't find a way to earn it myself."

Shannon didn't answer. She watched me write for a while. "You don't think I want you to go back north, do you?"

I shook my head. The thought had never occurred to me.

"I just don't understand what you're going to do," she said.

"I'm going to find a way to pay the rent and get the *Treasure Hunter*'s engines overhauled. Then I'm gonna salvage the *Dolphin*. And when school's over I'm going to dive outside the reef."

Shannon arched an eyebrow. "All by yourself?"

That made me smile. "You can come too."

That afternoon I went around the marina collecting bottles and jars. I was pretty sure I knew the trick to lying on broken glass. You lightly dulled all the sharp edges and points with an emery cloth first. I still wasn't sure about getting five tourists to stand on my back, but I figured I could start with one and work my way up.

I was sitting on the deck of the sailboat, breaking bottles with a hammer, when David Lester drove into the marina parking lot. He got out of the jeep and watched for a moment. "I was wondering what happened to that guy."

"I just hope he didn't bleed to death," I said, whacking another pop bottle.

David grinned. "Word is the shrimp are running tonight."

"Oh yeah?" I looked up at him.

"Yeah. And I could use some help with my net."

It was warmer that night than the last time I'd been on the railroad bridge. Most of the conchs were wearing shirts. They had their folding chairs, Coleman lanterns, and hibachis, but there were no open wood fires. The nets were leaning against the railing, and empty plastic buckets and pails were stacked in anticipation of the catch.

David was waiting for me near the middle of the bridge. His net was about five feet square. Other shrimpers were pressed close to him on either side, and I noticed Billy Peebles a few nets down. David had brought two folding chairs, a Coleman lantern, and a radio.

"How's it look?" I asked.

"Good," he said. "The tide's just starting. Trawler captains say they've been running big the last few days."

I leaned against the rail. The moon was almost full

against the midnight-blue sky, and a milky-white streak of light danced on the dark waves.

"Nice night," David said.

"Yeah."

"Just wait till about four this morning when your hands are like hamburger. You'll wish you'd never come."

"We'll see."

A little while later Shannon arrived. I'd had a feeling she was going to join us.

"Thought you'd have started by now," she said as she got off her bike.

"Just about to," David said.

The current picked up and people started to get ready.

"It's not too hard when the current's moving slow," David said as we lowered his net over the side and watched it sink into the dark water. "It gets tricky later. You don't stay in long enough, you won't get any shrimp. You stay in too long, the net gets so heavy, the rope'll snap when you try to bring it up."

"Heavy with shrimp?" I asked, picturing a hill of shrimp on the bridge pavement.

David just winked at Shannon and said, "You'll see."

Soon the Atlantic side of the bridge was full of nets, like kites floating down instead of up. Each net had plastic floats on the top edge and lead sinkers on the bottom to keep it vertical in the water. We leaned

against the railing, staring down at the current, waiting.

"Kinda boring, huh?" David asked, a teasing tone
in his voice.

Someone down the bridge brought a net in, and
word of his catch quickly moved along the rail.
" 'Bout two dozen small ones," said the man next to
us.

"Want to check ours?" I asked David. He tested the
rope with his hand and shook his head.

Five minutes passed and Billy brought his net in.
"Three dozen," he said. "Mostly small."

"Bait," David said.

Below us the water began to move faster. A net
came in a few yards from us. Two men flipped it over
the rail and spilled its contents onto the bridge. From
where I stood it looked mostly like seaweed and a few
small fish flopping around, but three people quickly
squatted next to the pile and started picking things
out.

"Okay, let's try it," David said.

I was amazed at how heavy the net felt as we
pulled it against the current. David put a foot against
the railing, and behind him Shannon and I pulled the
rope as if we were in a tug-of-war. Soon the net was
up to the railing. A dark ball of seaweed made its
center sag.

"Come on, Chris!" David yelled. I grabbed one
side of the net and together we lifted it over the rail

and dumped the contents. In the dark it looked like a big pile of wet leaves. David quickly lowered the empty net back into the water while Shannon brought the Coleman lantern close and started to spread the pile with a stick. Suddenly it came alive as dozens of shrimp flipped and bounced about.

"They're big!" she cried, plucking a plump, kicking shrimp out. I crouched down next to her. Small fish flopped around and crabs scampered for cover under the seaweed. I was reaching for a shrimp when an eel suddenly slithered out toward me. I jumped back, and Shannon and David laughed.

"Are there any more?" I asked, feeling embarrassed as I squatted down again.

"You never know," David said. He reached down and grabbed another big shrimp. Holding the body in his left hand, he twisted the head off. "Make sure the nerve comes out," he said, pointing to a thin black line hanging down from the head.

For the next five minutes we pulled heads off shrimp and divided the bodies into white buckets for small, medium, and large. Their shells were sharp and pointy, and soon my hands were covered with cuts. All along the bridge net after net came in and groups of people squatted in the lantern light, sorting the catch. By the time Shannon and I finished sorting and deheading our first netful, David was pulling another one in.

It was a long night—pulling the net, sorting, and

deheading. My hands were raw and bloody from the shrimp shells. At the peak of the tide, when the current was the fastest, we brought up all sorts of things —silver snappers, eels as thick as baseball bats, even a small sea turtle. That was when the biggest shrimp came in too. Ten inches long and as fat as a candy bar. People started hooting and hollering when they saw them.

By 3:30 the tide had slowed and we were bringing up fewer and smaller shrimp. The conchs began to pack up. They hauled their heavy pails of shrimp to the end of the bridge where their cars and pickups were parked. David and I shook out his net and coiled his rope. We had four and a half buckets.

"About a hundred and twenty pounds," he said as we hoisted the buckets into his jeep. We were taking the net apart when Billy passed, lugging two buckets. He dropped one behind the jeep.

"Here you go, snowbird," he said. In the dark I couldn't tell whether he was smiling or snarling.

"What's this for?" I asked.

"Christmas," he said, and trudged away.

It was after four when I got back to the sailboat and went to bed. Dad was snoring in his bunk. I slept till noon, and when I woke my hands were stiff and sore. After a while I went into the galley to see if there was anything for breakfast. On the table was an envelope with my name written on it. I rubbed my eyes and picked it up. It felt fat, but it didn't occur to me what might be inside until I opened it and a thick wad of bills fell out.

I was sitting at the table, staring at the money, when Dad came into the cabin. He must have gone out earlier that morning. "Where'd you get that?" he asked.

"Shrimping last night."

He sat down and thumbed through the bills. "Must've been a pretty good haul."

"I think I got more than my share," I said.

He gazed out the porthole. "Funny thing just happened to me too."

"What?"

"Went down to Lester's to have a look at the *Treasure Hunter*," he said. "Couldn't find her in the yard, so I started asking around and someone told me to go down to the dock. I found her in the water. New paint job, wood's all varnished, and her engines are done. There's a big blue tarp sitting on the dock next to her, and inside's all the diving and navigational equipment off the *Dolphin*."

"Someone salvaged it?"

"Peebles Marine Salvage," Dad said. "At least that's the name on the tarp. I went into the boat-yard office and asked to see the bills, and they said it was all taken care of."

He looked a little bewildered, which was understandable. For a moment I wondered if Tom and Betty had done it, but when I started adding up what

all that work must've cost, I knew it couldn't have
been them alone.

"Maybe I was wrong," I said. "Maybe people
around here do care."

Dad nodded but still looked puzzled and defeated.

"Listen to me, Dad," I said. "You know how Mom's
always worried that I'm gonna fall behind in my
homework because I'm too involved with treasure
hunting? Well, before Bobby died I had this speech in
my head I was going to give her the next time she
called. Now I think maybe you're the one who should
hear it. But I want you to really listen to me. I mean,
don't turn me off just because I'm your son, okay?"

For a moment Dad's expression started to change.
His bloodshot eyes began to narrow and the un-
shaved skin around his jaw tightened. I thought he
was going to get mad, but then he relaxed and nodded. He put his hands on the table and stared at
them. His fingers were gnarled and callused. The
knuckles were nicked and scarred.

"Dad," I began, "I never used to care whether we
found any treasure or not. I mean, I used to dive
because it was fun and I figured there was always a
chance we'd find something. But it was mostly a
game to me. Definitely never work. Maybe 'cause I
was a kid I never worried about money and fuel and
supplies. So it took a long time for me to realize that it
really was work for you. That you were the guy who
had to fix everything that broke, and who dived in

lousy weather because you couldn't afford to dive only on nice days, and who had to go out and beg investors for money. I realized that even when you find something you love, it still takes more work than you expect and longer hours than you want to spend.

"I watched you work for years, Dad. And you never quit. Even when things looked totally bleak you hung in and somehow they always got better. That's what I was going to tell Mom. That maybe I didn't do as well in school here as I would've if we'd stayed in Flintville. But I learned something I'd never have learned there. I learned that when you find something you love, you've got to stick with it no matter what. You can't ever give up. And if you work hard enough and long enough, you may not find all the treasure, but you'll find enough to get by."

Dad looked up at me, his eyes watery.

"You're a treasure hunter, Dad," I said. "You can't quit, because then you'd be nothing. *You* taught me that."

A tear ran down his cheek, but he was smiling. "I did, huh?"

I smiled back. "Yeah. And now that you've made me learn it, don't try telling me it isn't true."

23

The lesson Dad had taught me was a lot simpler in theory than in practice. Determined to start moving ahead again, we cleaned up the sailboat and made it more livable. But it still took Dad most of the spring to scrape together enough money to start diving.

When school ended I thought I'd gotten someone else's report card by mistake. The one I was looking at was filled with B's and C's. But it was mine. Almost every teacher had given me a higher grade than I deserved.

As summer vacation began we started diving outside the reef. Our progress was much slower than before. Where we'd once had three diving boats and nearly a dozen divers, we were back down to Dad, Shannon, and me. But soon we found a bronze astrolabe and some silver candlesticks, and Dad gradually came to believe that the *Sevilla* might again be within his reach. Still, the questions dogged us. How long could we go before we ran out of money again? What if another year passed and we still couldn't find the *Sevilla*?

That fall I started my senior year of high school and faced more tough choices. Mom was pushing hard for me to go to college. She thought she could get the money out of her father, but she said Keys Community College was out of the question. She didn't want me running off after classes each day to dive. Surprisingly, Dad agreed. If I wanted to keep diving, he said, I could come back during the summers.

By the end of September, Dad was almost broke again. I couldn't help him as much as I wanted because my guidance counselor said I needed really good grades that semester. I started spending my afternoons in the public library, away from the temptations of the sea.

One weekend in early October, Mom flew me up north to visit a couple of colleges. I got back late Monday night and found Dad waiting for me at the airport in Tom's pickup. In the back was all our stuff. Rents had been going up all over Key West, even for our leaky sailboat.

"Don't tell me we have to move again," I groaned.

Dad nodded.

I couldn't imagine what could be cheaper than that sailboat. A tent in the public campground?

"I rented a house on Flagler Avenue," Dad said.

I looked at him like he was crazy. Houses on Flagler must've rented for five times what we'd paid for the sailboat. Instead of explaining, Dad handed me a Polaroid snapshot. I held it up to the streetlight and squinted, but the photo had been taken underwater and it was dark and hard to distinguish. It looked like four old logs.

"Cannons, Chris," Dad said, grinning. "Off the *Sevilla*."

"You found her?" I gasped.

"I found her cannons. But for now that's fine."

Three-hundred-fifty-year-old cannons are as valuable as treasure as far as collectors and museums are concerned. The day after Dad found them he walked into the president's office at the First Bank of Key West, showed him the photos, and proceeded to borrow $25,000, using the cannons as collateral. After that, there was no doubt in my mind—he was his old self again.

After renting a second diving vessel and hiring three additional divers, Dad spent most of the winter bringing up more relics. We had a joke that he'd found every part of the *Sevilla* except the treasure. But behind the laughter was a serious concern. Was it just bad luck or was there a more compelling reason? In Spain, Julio was searching the archives again. It was crucial that the *Sevilla*'s treasure wasn't salvaged long ago.

I was accepted by three colleges that spring. Dad was happy for me, but I could tell he was sad too. Come September, I was finally going to leave.

By May at Key West High, senior slump was in full swing and I was diving every chance I got. I wanted to give it my best shot before leaving. One clear, calm morning I dived down to check a crater Dad was blowing near the reef. The crater was empty and I was about to swim back up when I noticed a large bump in the sand nearby. It looked like a car that had been buried under snow in a blizzard. As I got closer I saw the ends of several old timbers jutting an inch or two from the sand. The wood was black and so sodden that it came off in my hands when I touched it.

I swam back up and motioned Dad to move the *Treasure Hunter* over the spot.

"What have you got?" he asked.

"Can't tell yet," I said, and dived back down.

Dad moved the boat and turned the ducts on. I stayed below and watched the prop wash blow the sand away. I wish I'd had an underwater camera to record what I saw. As the sand was swept away something began to glimmer beneath it. A gold coin appeared. Then another and another. Soon a small mountain of gold and silver appeared. Parts of ancient treasure chests stuck out here and there, and it all rested on the blackened timbers of the *Sevilla*'s hull. When the sand was finally gone, I was staring at a pile of precious coins nearly five feet high.

I swam to the surface and pulled off my mask. Dad leaned over the gunwale and looked down at me. "So?"

"Can I get a car?" I asked.

Dad scowled, then broke into a wild grin. "Can we afford it?"

"No sweat," I said.

Dad made good on his word and paid off every investor, as well as all the divers who'd worked for him over the years. Shannon discovered she'd earned enough to go to college and graduate school if she wanted. Julio got enough so that he'd never have to research for students at the university again. And a big share went to Bobby Clark's family in St. Louis.

In town they even had a ceremony at which Dad

surprised everyone by announcing that he was donating one of the cannons and a number of other artifacts for permanent display in city hall. I think they would have made him an honorary conch that day if there was such a thing.

These days Dad and Mom have a house in Flintville and another in Key West. Mom quit the newspaper again, and she's writing an adventure-romance novel about a newspaper editor who's in love with a treasure hunter who searches the globe for sunken galleons. Lately she's been doing research for the book off the coast of Costa Rica, where Dad's new diving ship, the *Bobby Clark,* is searching for the wreck of the galleon that caught fire and sank in eight hundred feet of water.

And me? I go to a small college in the Midwest where no one's ever heard of the *Sevilla.* Shannon's at a large university about sixty miles north of here, and we see each other a lot on the weekends. I guess you could say we're more than "just friends." When school ends for the summer we'll both join the treasure hunt. The funny thing is, when my friends at school ask me what I'm doing for the summer and I tell them I'm going diving for sunken treasure off the coast of Costa Rica, they just laugh.

Lose yourself in award-winning teen fiction from

Laurel-Leaf books!

Exciting, action-packed adventures by

P.J. PETERSEN